A
SECOND CHANCE

Part of the
Pine City Chance Series

by

Marcella DiPaolo

ISBN: 978-1-64395-010-5 (Kindle eBook)
ISBN: 978-1-64395-110-2 (Paperback)

For copyright permission requests, or for information about special discounts available for bulk purchases, sales promotions, or educational needs, write to or e-mail the publisher at one of the following addresses.

Phantasy Publishing LLC
35 Brooks Drive
Bethalto, IL 62010

Website: www.phantasypublishing.com
E-mail: support@phantasypublishing.com

Published in the United States of America

Table of Contents

CHAPTER 1

1881
Pine City, Wyoming

It had been a long six months for Maggie McDonald. Her husband of ten years was killed in a poker game and while they had been living in the same house for the last nine of those years, they didn't share a bedroom or much of a life. Maggie remembered how happy they were when they first moved to Pine City after they were married. Stephen insisted on buying a large frame house on a quiet street on about an acre of land in the middle of the town. There were four bedrooms upstairs and another on the main floor. Maggie and Stephen planned on filling each of those bedrooms up with children. It didn't quite work out that way.

A year after they were married, Maggie found out that her loving husband was a liar, a cheat and a professional gambler. He had told her he was an investor, but he was really a con man milking men out of their money, one way or another. He had carried on countless affairs with other women while professing his love to her. And to make matters worse, he expected her to stay as his wife to present a respected front to the townspeople of Pine City. He said, after all, it's not like we'd be lying to anyone about their marriage, what goes on behind closed doors is nobody's business but theirs.

Maggie had heard enough lies. He was no longer welcome to her bedroom. She was going to open up her house and rent out rooms to boarders so that she would be able to pay the taxes on the property and still be able to live there. He could have one of the bedrooms, if he paid for the room at the beginning of each month just like everyone else. Stephen didn't like it, but he accepted the accommodations. Maggie cried a lot those first few years, but she held her head up high and looked the townspeople in the eye as she walked down the street. The same people that were judging her now knew about Stephen and they hadn't cared enough to tell her about it. She'd live her life and they could lead theirs.

She had managed to have the Sheriff and his Deputy stay in rooms at her home. The local teacher of their school also stayed in one of the rooms. Maggie made sure they were clean, their clothes were washed, ironed and returned the same day and meals were hot and appetizing. She had acquired a few friends over the years. They knew about Stephen and they supported her not him.

Olivia Clark, wife of Jonah Clark, helped run the General Store in town. Olivia and Maggie had been friends for years. Cade and Cate Murphy had actually lived in the same home town before they moved to Pine City. Maggie and Cate were friends until her death a year and a half ago. It was Maggie who helped Cade find another wife to help raise his five children.

Maggie's sister, Brenda Smith, lived in St. Louis, Missouri. She had a friend who had lost her husband and her little boy in a recent cholera epidemic. Brenda felt that Mary Williams would be the perfect wife for Cade and all those motherless children of his. Together, they arranged for the two to get together and wonder of wonders, they were extremely happy and also in love. Both Cade and Mary were very dear friends of hers.

She was a friend to Elizabeth Graham, one of Mary's neighbors and also Ava Drew, another of Mary's neighbors, but not as close as

Mary and Olivia were. When Stephen was shot over a poker game, they were the first to come forward to help her manage funeral arrangements and find a way to get over his death. Maggie didn't really mourn Stephen's death, she was sorry he was dead, but she'd cried nine years ago when she found out the kind of man she was really married to, she refused to cry at his funeral. She told them she refused to be a hypocrite, he had been dead to her for nine years and today was nothing new to her.

It was Cade and Mary who made her come out to their ranch and made her can vegetables and help with Mary's huge garden. The food she gained from them fed her the entire winter. Cade made sure she had smoked meat, flour and corn meal from his crops and smoke house. Their two oldest boys, Cam and Chris, brought in several wagonloads of chopped wood to keep her stove and fireplace warm. Olivia hired her to work several days a week in their store and in exchange she was able to get the remaining supplies she needed to keep her alive through the winter.

When her sister, Brenda, found out that she was now a widow, she took the train west to see her and spent several weeks in her home. When she came, she brought with her two of Mary's closest friends, Wes and Lily Peters. Wes was concerned how Mary was faring and they stayed several months before they returned to St. Louis as well. Wes was a U.S. Marshall and he was helping them get a new Sheriff and Deputy to come to Pine City. Their former Sheriff retired, and his Deputy was spending his time in the Territorial Penitentiary for killing Diana Scott. Diana was a neighbor of Cade and Cate's, but she wanted Cade. She proceeded to poison her husband and Cate in order to become Cade's next wife, he had other ideas. The Deputy was also in love with Cate and he couldn't stand by and let her killer go free. He shot her three times in the chest and then gave himself up to the local Sheriff. It was a mess!

But now, the Peters' had left, her sister had left, the Sheriff was gone and so was his Deputy. The teacher she had renting out a room, left to get married and take another job in another town. Her house was empty. She hated the silence and she really needed the money having boarders brought in.

When Stephen died, he actually had a winning poker hand and he had over one hundred dollars on him. Maggie received that money, but she didn't want to spend it unless she had too. The last telegram from Wes and Lily told her that the new Sheriff, his niece and his Deputy should be arriving any day. They planned to stay in her boarding house. Maggie knew she needed to start cleaning in preparation of their arrival, but the weather was so dreary, she couldn't bring herself to get started. She was so tired of her life and of her house and even the way she looked! She wanted a change. She just wasn't sure how to go about it.

She started making a list of what she would like to do about changing her house first. She needed to scrub all the floors in the bedrooms upstairs. They hadn't had new curtains in a very long time and that would help spruce them up and she needed to put different quilts on the beds instead of just colored blankets. She liked all those ideas, now what else?

She didn't want the hole under her house. She wanted a real cellar with wooden walls, floor and ceiling and she wanted to be able to get to it from her kitchen. She wanted to have some chickens and a cow. She loved getting eggs and butter from Mary and Cade, but she wanted her own animals. She also wanted her own garden where she could grow a lot of food to help feed her boarders and herself all summer, winter, spring and fall! She didn't know how she was going to get it all done, but she had a plan at last! She started heating up water to carry upstairs to start scrubbing. She even hummed while she worked.

It wasn't long after she began the floors; she had a knock at her front door. Her knees were wet from scrubbing, but she wiped the hair out of her eyes and went to the door anyway.

Mr. Hendricks from the railroad met her there. "Miz McDonald? I sure hate to bother you, but this here crate came in on the train yesterday, the wagons of supplies and deliveries came today, and it's addressed to you. I knew you didn't have any way to come and get it, so I loaded it on my wagon and brought it over. I hope that's all right?" Mr. Hendricks was dressed in jeans, a denim coat and a flannel shirt. He was bald as a chicken's egg on top of his head, but he had enough whiskers to reach to almost his waist.

"I sure appreciate you bringing it over, Mr. Hendricks. Is it very heavy or just bulky? Does it say anywhere where it came from or what it is?" Maggie asked him wondering how she was going to get it in her home and who sent it.

"I think the easiest thing to do is to take the crate apart and then carry whatever is in the crate into your house. You might not even want it in your house, maybe it'll go in the barn or the back porch." He scratched his head, "You don't happen to have a hammer do you that I could use?"

"As a matter of fact, I do! Let me go get it."

When she returned, Mr. Hendricks went to work. He had only taken three of the boards off, when Maggie took a huge breath! It was a sewing machine! Who would be sending her a sewing machine? They were expensive, and she didn't know anyone who had enough money to throw it away on a gift for her!

"Miz McDonald, it looks like there's an envelope tied to the machine. Give me a minute and I'll have the machine out and will be able to reach the letter." Sure enough, in five minutes the machine was out of the crate and carried into her parlor. Mr. Hendricks carried all the wood behind her house and put it in the

5

barn. He came back to the house to talk to Maggie. He liked being helpful to the little lady, she had a hard road ahead of herself.

Maggie ripped the envelope apart to find out who would be sending anything to her. It was from Brenda and George, her sister and brother-in-law! In one of the houses that they had bought and sold, this sewing machine was found. The new owner's or the old owners didn't want it, so they took it off their hands for a song. George helped her crate it up and get it on the train for Maggie. Brenda told her it was for all the Christmas's and birthdays she had missed over the years. She remembered how much Maggie liked to sew; maybe it could even help her make ends meet in her boarding house. Maggie was so happy, she started to cry. Thank you, Brenda and George, she had always wanted one but had never been able to afford it! Oh, the things she could make with the sewing machine!! Maybe things were looking up after all!!

That's when Mr. Hendricks made his move. He tried to put his arm around Maggie. Maggie was having none of it; she shoved her elbow into his stomach with as much muscle as she could muster. She also reached into the pocket of her apron and pulled out the little derringer that Mary had loaned to her.

"I'm getting pretty tired of being pawed by every single and some married men in this town, Mr. Hendricks! Just because I'm a widow doesn't mean I need or want your attentions! I have no inclinations of ever going to bed with any of you! Now get the Hell out of my house before I forget I'm a lady and shoot you where you stand!" Maggie was beside herself. She was so tired of being pitied by the people of this town, especially the people calling themselves the men of the town. They all felt she should be grateful for their attentions, her being a widow and probably lonely as well. Well, she wasn't any lonelier now than she had been for the last nine years living with that no-account husband of hers!

6

"Now, Miz McDonald, don't do anything rash with that there gun!" Mr. Hendricks said backing his way to the front door. "I know that little pea-shooter won't do no real damage..."

"Then you don't see where I'm aiming it at..." Maggie paused as suddenly Mr. Hendricks head snapped up and stared at her full in the eyes. Maggie's gun was pointed at his manhood! Why if she wasn't careful, she could shoot it clear off!

"Iffn' you shoot me, they'll put you in jail for shooting a law-abiding citizen!" He argued, talking very fast as he moved ever closer to the front door. He was going to try to make a quick get away!

Suddenly a new voice filled the room. It was harsh enough to make Mr. Hendricks jump in reaction. "If she shoots you, you'll be the one going to jail!"

"Who the hell are you!?" Mr. Hendricks asked in alarm.

"I'm the new Sheriff, that's who. I'm going to count to three and I better see you high tail it out of Miz McDonald's house and off her land. If not, she and I will both be shooting you for trespassing and harassment. Do I make myself clear?!" Maggie couldn't see him very well, he was in the shadow of the front door and porch, but she could tell he was big, and he had the meanest voice she had ever heard. She didn't know if she was glad or afraid that her boarders had arrived. Then she remembered what she had yelled at Mr. Hendricks before she knew that the Sheriff was at her front door, she was embarrassed and mortified that he should learn about her from yelling at a stranger. She blushed from the top of her head to the bottom of her feet. Whatever would he think about her now?

CHAPTER 2

Sam Kincaid was almost six-foot four and built like a bull. His Deputy, Reece McBride, wasn't much smaller. They had just arrived in town after traveling the five hours by horse from the railroad in Cheyenne, Wyoming. He was hot, dusty and in no mood to be nice to a grabby man who had just insulted his new landlady. He stared at Mr. Hendricks as he ran, not walked, to the wagon at the end of the walkway. He literally jumped into the wagon and fired up the mules that pulled it. He was gone within seconds of hearing that he was the Sheriff. Sam hadn't even gotten a good look at Miz McDonald yet, but he sure liked the look of her house.

His first sight of the light grey house was that it looked majestic sitting back a little way from the road. There was a walkway of a sort made out of rocks and there were flowers on either side of the walkway. It was too early for them to be blooming, but he could see bushes and carefully cared for flower beds all around her house. Two giant oak trees gave the front yard shade and he saw several more in her back yard. It looked to have a barn back behind the house and a smaller building as well. The light grey house had darker grey shutters and glass windows. Rockers sat on the front porch and a swing sat at the edge of the porch. It gave the entire place permanence and respectability. He wanted both for his niece. She had been through so much in the last several months.

Andie, her full name was Andrea, was named after his brother Andrew. Her mother had died in childbirth. Andrew had raised her by himself. She was a little bit of a thing, but she knew her Uncle Sam. He had stopped by often or as often as he could being a U. S.

Marshall. Andrew and Andie had lived in a boarding house on the end of town. It had caught fire one night. Andrew had gotten Andie out safely and then had gone back in to help save the others. He didn't make it out alive. Andrew had died a hero, but it didn't lessen the fact that Andie was now both motherless and fatherless.

Sam had gotten there as soon as he could. But he had never been married and had never been tempted. He didn't know the first thing about being a father or even being part of a family again. He felt at a loss dealing with Andie. His chance at a permanent job in Pine City seemed like the answer to his prayers. Here he and Andie could put down some roots and she could have a somewhat normal childhood.

Reece McBride had been his friend for many years. They had worked and hunted criminals for the last ten years. He was getting on in years; he wanted to sleep in a bed, a real bed every night, not sleeping on the hard ground. He wanted meals, good meals, three times a day, instead of eating beans heated out of a can at every meal. And he was tired, just plain tired of dealing with the dregs of society. Surely there had to be some good, honest people living out in all this vast country. He hoped to become friends with them and have a semblance of peace. Sam hoped to help him find it and at the same time find a place where he and his niece belonged.

Sam didn't miss much as he glanced in the door at Maggie. Her hair was falling down around her face. It was a deep sable color. And she had the bluest eyes he had ever seen. She also had the reddest face he had ever had the pleasure to witness. He figured she was embarrassed about the encounter he had had to see. He thought she showed spunk and outrage really well. She also looked like she could handle herself real well. He liked that in a woman.

"You are Miz Maggie McDonald?" Sam asked politely. "Wes told us you'd be expecting us, and we'd have a proper place to stay..." His voice faded away.

Maggie shook herself to get rid of her embarrassment. "Yes, I'm Maggie McDonald and I've been getting your rooms ready for you, that's why I look so bedraggled...Mr. Hendricks just brought over a crate that had arrived from the train from my sister and her husband. They're realtors in St. Louis and came across a used sewing machine. Brenda, my sister, knew I always wanted one, so they sent it cross country to me." She paused, she realized that she was blabbering, she was sure that neither Sam nor his Deputy cared less whether she was now the proud owner of a sewing machine. "I just finished scrubbing the floors in the bedrooms and the sheets are on the line. I'll make up the beds as soon as they're dried. If you'll follow me, I'll show you the rooms."

Maggie walked around the three in her entryway and started walking up the staircase to the second floor of her house. Everywhere Sam looked, he could see the gentle touch of Maggie. The walls were freshly painted and there were pictures hanging on the wall. Doilies were on the end tables in the parlor and a rug lay in front of a couch and two very comfortable looking chairs. They all faced the fireplace and mantle. On the mantle were a majestic looking wooden clock and two candles. This is the kind of homey atmosphere he wanted for Andie, Sam thought.

There were four bedrooms upstairs, two on each side of the hallway. At the end of the hallway there was a closet. Sam assumed that it was a linen closet. All four rooms looked to be furnished exactly the same. There was a bed with a mattress, an armoire with two drawers and to doors above them. Sam assumed that there were hooks and a rod to hang up their clothes inside the small doors of the armoire. There was also a small table where a pitcher and a basin stood to wash in. A small mirror hung on the wall above the basin. The windows were bare, but privacy was available in the shades that were above each of the windows. The rooms smelled clean with a trace of lye soap still in the air. The walls were all painted white and the wood floors were a dark brown that glistened from the scrubbing that Maggie had just given them. With a nod at Reece, Sam turned to his niece.

"Reece and I will take the two rooms facing the town. Andie, which room do you want?" He asked quietly. Andie just shrugged her shoulders. "Well, if you don't have any preference, let's put you in the room across from mine. How's that sound?"

Andie nodded her head. She didn't care where she went. Nothing would ever bring her Pa back to her. As far as she was concerned, nothing would ever be right in her world again.

Maggie spoke into the silence. "If you'll put your saddle bags and luggage into the proper rooms, when I make up the beds, I'll put them in the drawers and hang things in the armoire for you. I planned to make some curtains for the windows. With the sewing machine, I'll hope to get them up today or tomorrow at the latest..." She hesitated, "Andie would you like to go with me to the General Store to pick out the color you wanted for your room's curtains?"

Andie thought of the words of the lady in front of her. She had sounded kind, not like some of the ladies where she and her dad had stayed. They all pretended to like having her around, when all they really wanted was to get her Pa to marry one of them so they could take care of them. This lady hardly glanced at Uncle Sam and Reece. She nodded her head; it might be fun to actually pick out the color of curtain for her window.

Sam smiled; he was glad that Andie would be taken care of for a couple of hours at least so that he and Reece could go over to the jail and see what they were dealing with. "Miz McDonald, the rooms look real nice and that bed will sure feel good tonight for all of us. Would it be all right with you, if Andie stayed with you for a little while this afternoon, so that Reece and I can get our horses settled and see what problems there are that we need to know about?"

Maggie smiled for the first time since they had met, but she was smiling at Andie while she spoke. "I would love to have Andie accompany me to the store and then maybe she wouldn't mind helping me make some dinner for all of us. Would you mind spending some time with me Andie?"

Andie was puzzled; she was asking her not her Uncle Sam. She was actually going to have a say in what she would be doing today. She nodded and smiled at Maggie. It might be fun to be able to go to the store and she always liked being in a kitchen, even if she had never been able to help cook. Maybe this kind lady really liked children and wouldn't mind having her around.

"Good, "Her uncle told them all together, "Now I have another question to ask you...or rather several questions to ask you. Who is the mayor of this town? I need to get in touch with him to let him know we've arrived and to get the badges that Reece and I will wear." He hesitated again, "I hate to ask, but when you're getting curtain material, would you mind finding some clothes for Andie? Everything she owned was lost in the fire. She only has the clothes on her back. I really don't know what to buy or what size..." Again, his voice faded away. He was asking an awful lot of a lady he just met a few minutes ago.

"Jonah Clark is the mayor of the town and also the owner of the General Store. If you'll follow me and Andie to the store, I'll introduce you and then get some clothes for Andie. It'll be fun spending someone else's money for a change! There is a resale shop in town that sells clean gently used clothing if you don't mind." Maggie didn't want to hurt his feelings about buying used over new, but she had been so used to saving every penny she could get her hands on, it was second nature to assume that everyone needed to save their money.

"That would be great." Sam breathed a sigh of relief. Maggie McDonald seemed to be just the sort of landlady they needed to get them set up and feeling like they were home at last. "Let me and Reece give you the rent for the month and then I'll give you money to spend on Andie, as well. How much is the rent?"

"I charge five dollars a month. That includes two meals a day here, but I'll send a sack lunch with you for your noon meal. I'll also wash your clothes and keep your rooms clean. Does that sound fair to you?" Maggie sure hoped so, she needed the money.

"More than fair..." They both answered. Reece gave her a five-dollar gold piece and Sam gave her three five-dollar gold pieces. At her questioning look, he told her, "Spend the rest on Andie, I have no idea how much it costs to get her what she needs. If it costs more, just let me know."

Maggie nodded her head, loving the feel of the money in her hand. Everything was going to be all right, she just knew it was.

CHAPTER 3

Maggie disappeared into her own bedroom on the first floor for a few minutes. She came out looking a lot better. She had changed into a dry skirt and had redone her hair. She picked up her purse and placed the four five-dollar gold pieces in it and joined her new boarders by the stairs.

"Maybe I should show you around the bottom floor, too, before we leave for the General Store." She began. "Just like there are four bedrooms upstairs, there are four rooms down here as well. This is the parlor and you are welcome to sit by the fire anytime you wish, in here is the dining room. I will serve you breakfast and dinner here. My bedroom is the first room to your right and down this hall is the kitchen. You'll notice the small room in the corner. There is a bath tub in there. We heat up water here on the stove reservoir and carry it by the bucketful to the tub. After you're done, you get to empty the tub with those same buckets. I usually encourage my boarders to pour the water on any of my flowers around my house. It saves me the trouble of watering them myself, any questions?"

"Why do we eat in the dining room instead of the kitchen table?" Sam asked.

"It's just always been done that way; how would you like it to be?" Maggie asked.

"Do you join us for dinner in the dining room?"

"No...I usually serve my boarders and eat in the kitchen when they're done. Why do you ask?"

"Well, I think it's pretty silly to have us eat in there and you eat in here all by yourself." He began, "I think we should all sit down together in the kitchen. We're not fancy people, I think we'll feel more at home in the kitchen and I personally think it's a lot of extra work on your part to have to serve us in the other room. Is that all right with everyone?" He looked at Reece and he nodded and then at Andie. She smiled at him for the first time today.

"I think I'd like that, Uncle Sam." Andie told him.

"Then it's been decided! That is if it's all right with Miz McDonald..."

"I...I'd like that. I would like to share my meal with all of you. Thank you for making my job easier, Sheriff Kincaid." Maggie told him and smiled at him for the first time. Her blue eyes almost looked like she had a tear in them. For the first time in nine years, she wouldn't be eating alone.

It didn't take them any time at all to walk to the jail and to the General Store. Maggie introduced Sam, Reece and Andie to Jonah Clark, owner of the store and Mayor to Pine City.

"Welcome to Pine City! We are sure glad you came here to Pine City, we heard a lot of good things about both of you from Wes Peters before he left to go back home. I've got your badges right here waiting for you; all we got to do is make this official by having you sworn in. Olivia! Can you spare us a few minutes to act as a witness and Maggie would you act as my other witness?" Jonah asked wiping off his hands on his white apron.

"Can Andie be a witness, too, Jonah? Sam is her Uncle..." Maggie asked hoping to make her feel a part of the ceremony.

"That would be perfect, "Jonah told her. "Andie, after these two men make their sworn statements, you hand them their badge, OK? The gold one goes to the Sheriff, your uncle and the silver one goes to Mr. McBride. Maggie and Olivia, if you would both face the two officers...I think we're set. Now raise your right hand and repeat

15

after me...I solemnly swear to uphold the office of Sheriff and Deputy of Pine City to the best of my ability..." He waited for both men to say the pledge before he continued..." I Promise to keep my own biases and prejudices out of doing what's right for the town. I solemnly swear, so help me God." Both Sam and Reece repeated the promise and then Andie handed them each their badges.

"Well, that's that. How else can I help you guys out?"

"Well, Mayor, we were wondering if you have a map of the surrounding area for starters. Secondly, do we collect a fee from the local businesses and anyone who wants to start up a business? Thirdly, when can we expect the circuit judge to come to town to hear any and all charges on anyone in my jail? And fourth, how much help can we expect from the citizens of Pine City should we run into trouble?" Sam asked.

"Olivia, why don't you help Maggie get what she needs while I answer their questions. I may even go over to the jail and make sure everything is in order for them. Sheriff, here are the keys to the jail and to the cells in the back of the jail..." Jonah's voice trailed away as he led Sam and Reece back to the jail to answer their questions.

"What can I do for you today, Maggie?" Olivia asked her friend.

"We need some material to make curtains for all the bedroom windows. I want them to look more welcome. And then Andie and I are going to go to the resale shop and get her some clothes. I will also need a ham and a good-sized roast; it can be of venison or beef. I will also need a dozen eggs and a pail of milk." Maggie told with a smile. She glanced down at Andie, "What color did you want for your room?"

Andie shrugged her shoulders. She had no idea what color she wanted, now what would they do?

"No problem, let's go look at the selection. Maybe, one of the patterns will grab your interest!" Maggie grabbed Andie's hand

and walked over to the material. There were over twenty different bolts of cloth in all kinds of colors! Andie looked at all of them and ran her hand over the soft cotton material. She finally stopped in front of small white and purple flowers.

"Would this one be all right? I really like the color purple..." Andie asked in a quiet voice.

"Absolutely! I like that pattern, too. It'll look nice on the windows and we should have enough left over to cover the pillows on your bed, too." Maggie told her. "We'll need at least four yards of that, Liv and I think the white eyelet for the other windows. You'll probably need to give me at least nine yards of it. While you get the rest of our order done, we're going next door to the resale shop. We'll be back to pay and pick up the purchase, all right?"

"That should just give me enough time to measure this out and cut the roast! Have fun picking out some pretty clothes!" Liv waved them on and started measuring out the material for the curtains.

The resale shop was actually across the street from the General Store. Maggie knew the owner and greeted her as she and Andie entered the store. "Grace, you're just the person we needed to see. Andie's clothes were lost in a fire, so we need to get her an entire wardrobe. Could you show us where her size might be?"

"Why, I'd be delighted in helping you out Maggie! Let's see, I think you'll find her sizes on these tables. Shoes are probably stacked under the table. Have her try them on to make sure they fit. I'll let you shop and if you need me, I'll just be at the front counter." Grace walked back up to the front of the store giving them time to sort through the clothes.

"Andie, what do you say to a couple of dresses, a couple of pinafores, some petticoats, bloomers, socks, a nightgown, shoes and a jacket?" Maggie looked at Andie to see if she agreed. "That should get us started and give you something to choose from each morning. I would probably also suggest another pair of pants and a shirt. My friend Mary always asks me to go berry picking with her when the berries get ripe in the woods by her house. Her daughter always wears pants to go. She says it's a lot easier than wearing a dress."

"Do we have enough money to buy all of that Miz McDonald?" Andie was amazed at the amount of clothes she had listed.

"We sure do Andie! Now help me choose colors that you like and will like wearing, all right?"

Much to Andie's delight they found a purple print dress and a lilac pinafore and a yellow gingham dress with a white pinafore. She liked the navy pants and plaid shirt they picked out and the shoes were a lot lighter than the boots she had on now. They found a nightgown that was white with purple flowers embroidered around the edge of the collar and the sleeves. The coat was a light grey. She even liked the petticoats and bloomers, Maggie helped her find. Because every dress or article of clothing was only five cents the shoes a dime, Maggie spent less than a dollar getting her outfitted.

"Ma'am?" Andie told her hesitantly, "My Uncle Sam only had one pair of pants and another shirt, do you think we have enough money to buy him some clothes, too?"

"We sure do and his deputy too! This way if they get caught in the rain, they will always have clean, dry clothes to change into. That's good thinking Andie. Let's see if we can find their sizes. Your uncle is a big man and so is his deputy!" Maggie and Andie both laughed.

They found what Maggie hoped would fit the two men and quickly purchased two pairs of pants and two shirts for each of them. Then they grabbed two pair of long johns for each of them. Maggie had Andie count out six pairs of socks for the men and they headed up to pay for their purchases. On the way, Maggie noticed some used rag dolls on one of the tables; one of them was dressed in a purple dress. Maggie grabbed it as they passed. Andie couldn't believe all that Maggie had purchased and then she gave her the doll. Andie had lost her dolls in the fire. She hugged the little doll to her and then reached out and hugged Maggie.

"Thank you, Miz McDonald! I've been missing my doll from the fire. I'm so glad we'll be living in your house with you!" Andie told her against her shoulder.

"Not as glad as I am Andie! And since we're going to be such good friends, I think you should just call me Maggie, not Miz McDonald. What do you think?" Maggie asked her, feeling as happy as Andie was.

"I'd like that a lot...Maggie!" Andie told her and gladly took the package holding all her new clothes and her new doll. Maggie picked up the rest and together they went across the street to get the rest of their shopping and go home. It was a good beginning for both of them.

CHAPTER 4

As soon as Maggie and Andie arrived back at the boarding house, Maggie put the roast in the oven to start it cooking. She had Andie help her get all the dry sheets off the line and together they started making up the beds. Maggie took Andie downstairs to her own bedroom and opened up a large trunk that she had under the window. Inside were quilts of just about every color and pattern. Maggie had had a lot of spare time over the last nine years and making quilts helped her fill that time up. Now they were going to be put to good use.

Andie chose a blue one in a Log Cabin pattern for her Uncle Sam's room and a patchwork quilt of every color she could imagine for Mr. McBride. Under all the quilts, they found one she fell in love with; of course, it was all different colors of purple in a Granny's Fan pattern. They took them upstairs and immediately put them on the beds. With the blanket they had already put on the beds, her boarders would be very warm. Then they hung and put away all the clothes they had bought, even those of Sam's and Reece's. Taking them out of their saddle bags and putting them in the drawers, made them seem more permanent.

There were still several hours until dinner time, so Maggie had Andie help her peel some potatoes and carrots to add to the roast. Andie loved Maggie's kitchen. It had yellow gingham curtains and a yellow checked oilcloth on the table. Yellow was Andie's second favorite color. It also smelled really good with the roast cooking and four loaves of freshly baked bread on the counter. Maggie made sure she had a large slice with butter on it as they worked.

Then she started on the curtains. Of course, she made up Andie's first. It took no time at all to hem the cloth and make a hem to put the dowel rod through to hang them in her room. She also made up a pillow case in the same material just like she promised. Before they hung them, Maggie quickly made up curtains for all three of the other bedrooms. They started a batch of cookies for dessert and ran upstairs to hang the curtains before dinner was ready.

Andie loved her purple room! She also felt Sam's and Reece's room looked a lot better with curtains hanging from the windows. Best of all, she had had fun being with Maggie today. She didn't feel she was in the way and Maggie had a way about her that made her feel she was really helping. She liked that a lot. She couldn't wait for Sam and Reece to get home to show them their new bedrooms. Not to mention, she also couldn't wait to eat some of the good food Maggie was making in the kitchen!

Sam and Reece had had a busy day. They both walked up and down the sidewalks introducing themselves to each and every store in the entire town. Tomorrow they hoped to ride out and visit the surrounding ranches and farms so they would get a feel for the land and its people. So far, they rather liked what they saw and who they met. There were only a few people that they didn't get a warm welcome from. Michael Hunt from the First National Bank of Pine City seemed a little pompous to both of them, while Bart Murray of the Pine City Bank seemed like an all right guy.

To each place of business they announced that they would tolerate no shooting in town, they wouldn't make the ranchers and farmers leave their weapons at the jail, but they were to be used for protection only. They especially made it clear to the saloon owners that they wanted to make Pine City a quiet and hopefully prosperous town. Every single man and woman agreed with them.

The town was impressed with the size of the two men and of their quiet presence. They were really glad they had finally arrived. They would all rest easier at night knowing that they had a Sheriff and a Deputy again to keep the peace in town.

One of the things that Jonah Clark had given them was a map of the town and the surrounding area. He pointed out where they had found rustlers in the past, where there were hidden caves near the river, where Indians still hunted and where they could expect any trouble. He also promised that the town would pay ten cents a day to feed any prisoners they captured and if a posse were necessary, several men in town would help them out. Everything they learned helped them like the town a little bit more. They sure liked the mayor, he told it to them straight, no sugar coating involved. He also gave Maggie high marks as a cook and landlady. Just hearing him talk, made them want to get home to a well-cooked meal all the more. Sam worried about Andie. He had left her in the hands of a virtual stranger and Andie didn't like too many people. He hoped they had gotten along well. He had hoped to enlist Maggie's help in watching Andie each day as he worked, but he didn't know how much that was going to run him. With the livery bill and rent, there wasn't going to be a lot left over from his paycheck each month.

They arrived home to find Andie and Maggie sitting on the front porch in the swing. Sam was surprised to see Andie talking and laughing. She'd been very quiet since Andrew's funeral, too quiet. He didn't know what he could do to make her feel more like her old self again. Seeing her laughing with Maggie, looked like the old Andie he remembered. He was grateful to Maggie for making her feel so at home.

"Uncle Sam! Uncle Sam! Guess what?" Andie shouted jumping from the swing and running to meet her Uncle.

"I give up, what?" Sam scooped up Andie and gave her a hug and a kiss on her cheek. He loved seeing her so happy.

"I got a purple room! Can you believe it?? Maggie helped me find clothes and a purple doll just like the one that got burned up in the fire and we even found a purple quilt to put on my bed. Wait till you see it!" Andie paused for breath, "Come see your rooms, me and Maggie fixed them up, too! Maggie put the rest of your money on your table in your room. We even picked up some shirts and pants for you and Reece, so you'd have dry clothes if you get caught in the rain! Hurry! Then we got a real good meal in the kitchen and guess what?" Not waiting for an answer, she hurried on, "Maggie even let me help make dinner! I wasn't in the way! I think she likes me, Uncle Sam!"

Sam was unprepared to hear that they had spent money on clothes for him, too. But upon hearing that they had money left over, he gave a sigh of relief. He could sure use the extra clothes, that's for sure. He couldn't remember the last time he had put on clean clothes. It would sure feel good to take a hot bath tonight and stretch out in that bath tub, Maggie had mentioned. He had to make sure that Andie had a bath as well.

As soon as Sam and Reece walked into the boarding house, they could smell the aromas from the kitchen. Their stomachs grumbled as they followed the excited Andie up the stairs. They looked in Reece's room first as it was the first one, they came to in the hall. Having curtains on the window and a colorful quilt on the bed, transformed the austere bedroom into a welcoming warm room that beckoned them to spend some time. Sam's room was every bit as warm as Reece's and he liked the shirts and pants they had picked out for each of them. Andie's room was perfect. The colorful curtains and the quilt with the purple ragdoll lying on the pillow, made Sam smile. This was what he wanted for Andie; someplace she could feel at home in. Andie even opened her

Armoire to show him all her new clothes. Sam was surprised at how much Maggie had bought and still had enough to buy some much needed clothes for he and Reece and he didn't forget that his change was on the little table in his room.

Sam and Reece washed up in their bedrooms in the basin and pitcher on the tables. Then all three of them hurried downstairs to the kitchen to eat dinner. The feast on the table brought them up short. She had made enough food to feed an army! Reece and Sam quickly sat down, but not before Sam held the chair for Maggie and for Andie. Maggie reached for each of the hands of the people next to her. Everyone else followed suit.

Maggie prayed, "Bless us Lord for this food and to the new boarders you brought to my doors. We thank you for all our blessings, Amen." When she looked up, she was staring into Sam's face. He mouthed the words, "Thank you!" before he started filling his plate and Andie's. Maggie gave a huge sigh of relief. She wasn't feeling so lonely after spending the day with Andie and eating a meal with her boarders. She had hopes to call them friends in the very near future. It was a wonderful ending to an eventful day.

It seemed strange to be engaged in conversation while eating dinner. Maggie had spent so many years virtually alone, that the noisy talking was enjoyed. "Did Jonah Clark answer all your questions, Mr. Kincaid?" Maggie asked him.

"He was great. Showed us where every shop in Pine City is located and then Reece and I went around and introduced ourselves to everyone. We hope to go out to all the ranchers and introduce ourselves to them tomorrow." Sam told her.

"Oh, would you mind giving the Murphy's a message for me when you talk to Cade and Mary?" Maggie asked quickly.

"Sure, between Reece and me, we should be able to remember it. What is it you wanted to tell them?"

"Their older boys, Cam and Chris, chopped all my firewood last year. I was hoping that they would bring some more in for me and also bring in their dad's plow. I was hoping that they would plow up a patch of ground for Andie and me to plant a garden..." Maggie told him.

"You mean it, Maggie? You'd let me help with planting the seeds and weeding and picking the vegetables and everything?" Andie was overjoyed on hearing that her time spent with Maggie wasn't ending.

"I'm counting on your help Andie!" Maggie laughed. "Mary Murphy has five children and all of them helped her plant her garden and helped her maintain it. She canned a whole cellar full of food that they ate all winter and gave me enough to eat as well. I'm going to plant a garden and can as much as I can. With Andie's help, I'm pretty sure we can do it! Do you mind her helping me?"

"I'm thrilled that she wants to help. I was...going to ask you...if you would mind keeping an eye on Andie while I'm working. If you're too busy, I understand, and I'll ask around and see who I can find. I will pay you for your time..." Sam's voice stopped when he looked up and saw that Maggie was angry.

"You will not pay me for the time I get to spend with Andie. I loved having her with me today and I would love to have her company every day. But I would ask that as you go see the ranchers and farmers that if you see a deer or a turkey or even a wild hen, to shoot it. The meat will help out at our meals and that way it saves you money and me too." Maggie told him in no uncertain terms.

"How are you going to store the meat?" He questioned.

"I have a smoke house in the rear of our property. It hasn't been used for a long time, but I thought that while I have Andie, we could clean it out and use it. What do you think Andie, does that sound like something you'd like to help me with?" Maggie asked her to try to include her in the decision process.

"It sounds like fun. I bet we get really dirty cleaning out that old smoke house, won't we?" Andie grinned while eating another helping of carrots.

"Miz McDonald that would be great, as long as you're sure about this. Reece and I will love filling up that smoke house for you and we'll take care of cutting it up and skinning it too. Is that all right with you Reece?" Sam asked him.

"I'll shoot anything that moves if we get to eat like this every night! Ma'am that was sure good eating. I thank you for the vittles and the company. I really like the way you and Andie fixed up our rooms. I feel like I'm in my own house instead of just renting a room. I appreciate all you done to make us feel welcome, especially the extra pants and shirts. You're taking real good care of us and it's not going unnoticed!" Reece told her, "One last thing, how about you call us Sam and Reece instead of Mr. Kincaid or Mr. McBride; we do live in the same house after all?"

"I'd like that...Reece and I insist that you call me Maggie not Mrs. McDonald." Maggie smiled at both men. This was going to work out really well after all, Maggie thought.

CHAPTER 5

Sam, Reece and Andie all took hot baths while Maggie washed and dried the dishes from dinner. Sam and Reece also took care of filling the tub and emptying it out on her flowers just like she talked about. Andie looked really cute in her new nightgown and she kissed Maggie goodnight as she ran up the stairs to bed. For the first time in a long time, Andie was looking forward to waking up in the morning. She couldn't wait to get dirty cleaning out the smokehouse with Maggie or planting a garden.

Sam and Reece didn't stay up long before they went up to bed too, but before he did, Sam wanted to tell Maggie thank you for all she had done for Andie and for he and Reece as well. He didn't want her to think she was unappreciated. He was thrilled that Andie would have someone who really wanted to spend time with her looking after her. Shooting game instead of paying someone would save him some money and help out Maggie as well. It was a win-win situation as far as he was concerned. He found Maggie in the parlor getting ready to sew on her new sewing machine.

"Maggie...I just wanted to tell you thank you for all you've done for all of us today. I really appreciate how good you've been to Andie...she's seemed kind of lost since her dad died. Today was the first time since his death, that I saw her animated and laughing so natural. She was more like her old self. I know that buying her clothes or making her curtains and even letting her help get supper ready weren't what you signed up for with us being boarders and all. I just really am grateful for all you're doing watching Andie..." Sam told her with his hat in his hands.

"Sam you don't need to tell me thank you, it's I who should be thanking you and Andie. Do you have any idea of how many meals I've eaten alone in the last nine years? Or how often I'm alone? Andie was like a breath of fresh air today. She's a wonderful little girl and I truly loved having her keep me company. I am really looking forward to having her help in the smokehouse and the garden. I hope you don't mind me taking her with me when I go out to the Murphy's to pick berries in a week or so. They have a daughter, Kit, who's about Andie's age; I think they'll get along really well. It would be nice for Andie to have someone to play with; I'll make sure she's introduced to other children her age so she can pick and choose her friends. Above all, I want her happy. I'll do whatever I can to make sure that happens. Thank you for bringing so much sunshine into my house, Sam, I really appreciate you getting meat for us and letting me eat with you at mealtimes. It means a lot to me." Maggie told all of this to Sam with her head bowed over her sewing. She finally looked up with tears in her eyes. Sam was overcome with the urge to gather her up in his arms to offer some comfort, but he remembered how she reacted when Mr. Hendricks tried to touch her this afternoon. He nodded his head, said good night and went on up to bed. She had given him a lot to think about.

They were all awakened when the pounding started on the front doors around one o'clock in the morning. Several men who had drunk too much were pounding on the doors asking for Maggie to let them in. They'd be glad to keep her company! "Let us in Miz McDonald! We'll see that you have a high old time between the sheets with all of us!" That's when Sam and Reece opened the door with both of their six-guns drawn.

"Boys, I am the new Sheriff of Pine City and this is my new Deputy. We don't take kindly to being woken up by the pounding of the door and men who should know better than yelling at a widow lady. You have two choices. You can leave and promise never to come back, or we lock you up in the jail to dry out and cool down. I think the circuit judge comes in about two weeks. You'd be our guests until then. Make your choice. I'd like a little more sleep before I resume my duties as Sheriff." Sam told the astonished men.

"Our apologies...we won't be back...Come on guys, I told you it was a dumb idea to begin with..." The three men stumbled away back towards town. Sam and Reece holstered their weapons and headed back upstairs. That's when Sam saw Maggie standing by the staircase holding a shotgun in her hands. He could tell by her red face that she was embarrassed. But she was a sight to behold in her white nightgown and her glorious hair hanging down her back. Her eyes were flashing, she was mad all right.

"I'm sorry you and your deputy had to deal with the scum of our little town. They've started coming around ever since Wes left. They seem...to think...that I'm lonely and would encourage their company. I don't and never will! I was just going to open the door and let loose with the shotgun. It's only got bird seed in it, but it would have gotten the idea across that I'm tired of being bothered by every one of them. I thank you for your interference. Good night." Maggie turned around and almost ran to her own bedroom. Sam watched her go and smiled. Maggie sure had grit, that's for sure.

Morning came and with it came the smells of bacon frying as the two men came down the stairs together. Andie was still asleep in bed. Maggie had biscuits and gravy and fried bacon ready for them. She had also made up two small packages of biscuit and bacon sandwiches for them to take with them for lunch. Reece smiled and told her they would not go to waste! They left shortly afterwards. They had looked really nice in the clothes that they had bought for them yesterday. Maggie went upstairs to make their beds and get all their dirty clothes to wash. She immediately started heating water to wash the dishes and the clothes.

When Andie came downstairs, she was wearing her new pants and shirt. If they were going to get dirty, she didn't want it to be on her new dresses! Maggie had saved some biscuits and gravy for her and she ate with gusto. You would have thought that she hadn't eaten in days! While she ate, Maggie changed into her own pants and shirt. She washed up Andie's dishes and helped her make her bed and the two of them headed outside to clean out the smokehouse.

It had been several years since they had used it. Stephen, Maggie's late husband, had not felt the need to plan ahead. He didn't see the need to plant a garden or gather meat or even keep the barn in good shape. This was Maggie's, so the work and the upkeep was hers too. She was the one to paint the house and plant the flowers. She struggled each month to have enough money to have enough food for her and her boarders. Stephen gave her no money for taxes or anything, just the five dollars rent she asked from each of her boarders. It was no wonder that Maggie had never counted on anyone except herself to get anything done. It was fun having someone to talk to and laugh with.

Together the two pulled out all the limbs and twigs that had accumulated over the years. Maggie actually swept out the dirt floor to get rid of all the leaves. She also used that broom to sweep down all the cobwebs they found hanging from the ceiling! Ugh! They both hated the thought of spiders getting in their hair or climbing over their clothes. They checked each other over carefully to make sure that neither one of them had any unwanted visitors on themselves!

It was while they were finishing the smokehouse that Andie thought she saw someone or something moving in the barn. Maggie didn't think there was anything in the barn other than a lot of mice, but together they decided to check it out. Maggie still had her derringer in her pocket, and they were quiet as they approached the open barn door.

Maggie looked into the barn for the first time in a long time. At one time, it housed several horses and even a cow. But they had long since been sold to pay off Stephen's gambling losses. Now it was just a big, empty building. Maggie didn't even know if there were any straw left in the loft. The barn itself smelled musty and dirty. Andie sneezed twice just from the dust motes they stirred up. She had just decided to leave when she heard the boards in the loft squeak, as if someone were walking on them.

Maggie pulled her derringer and pushed Andie behind her, "Whoever is up in the loft, come down. I have a gun pointed right at you and won't hesitate to shoot!" Steps crossed over the loft and finally a barefoot started to climb down the ladder leading up to the loft.

"Don't shoot Ma'am, I mean you no harm!" The voice came from a small grey-haired black man. He was wearing clothes that were too large on his small frame and had no shoes to speak of. "I just climbed up in the loft to get a few hours' sleep before I moved on. I didn't take nothing..."

"What's your name?" Maggie asked shocked to see anyone really come down from the loft. "Where are you from?"

"The name's Silas...just Silas. I was a slave down south. When the war ended, I just left the plantation and tried to find work. If there was work, I stayed a while. If there wasn't no work, I moved on. I heared tell of land out west for anyone who wanted some. I thought I'd try and get me some. But a lot of land is already taken, and I got no way of getting the tools to farm the land or make me a house. So I was just tryin' to land me a job, and git me enough food to eat and keep body and mind together." Silas told her with as much dignity as he could muster.

"Are you hungry?" Maggie asked lowering her derringer from pointing it at him. "Andie and I were just getting ready to go in and make us some sandwiches. Would you like to join us?"

"That would be real nice, Ma'am, but I don't want to put you out none." Silas told her. He wasn't used to being asked to eat with two white women ever!

"Come on in and wash up Andie and I are filthy getting that old smokehouse cleaned out, so we could use it again. What kind of work do you do, Silas?" Maggie led the way into her kitchen and washed her hands and helped Andie wash hers. She turned the sink and warm water over to Silas so he could enjoy the soap too. He actually closed his eyes as he washed his face and his hands. It was as if using warm water was a luxury he wasn't used to. Maggie ushered him to sit down and poured him some tea and gave him two sandwiches of bread and roast beef. She fixed Andie a sandwich of roast beef and one for herself too. They ate in silence for a few minutes and then Silas answered her.

"I do a little bit of everything. I worked on the crops on the plantation and I've worked in liveries sometimes and once I even got a job helping out a carpenter. I really like working with wood and building something where there weren't nothing there before. I guess you could say I was a jack of all trades and master of none."

Maggie's mind was working a mile a minute. Silas could be the answer to her prayers. He could help her build a cellar without snakes and he could help her build a chicken coup and fix up the barn again. She couldn't pay him much, just room and board and some used, clean clothes and shoes, Maggie thought.

"Silas, would you be agreeable to working here for a while? I want to clean up the barn, build a chicken coup, get a cow and build a corral. Would you be interested in helping me out?" She hurried on to add, "I can't pay you anything, but I can offer you a warm place to sleep, clean clothes and three meals a day. We'll see about what else we need done when those jobs are completed. Are you interested?" Maggie held her breath.

"Why, I'd be glad to work for you! I don't need no pay Iffn' I got me food to eat and a place to stay. Did you say clean clothes? I ain't got nothing but the clothes on my back..." Silas told her.

"Well, that's going to be one of our first stops, the clothing store. We're going to get you several pairs of pants and shirts, long johns, socks, shoes, a jacket, suspenders and a hat. We're also going to go to the lumber yard and order some wood to start on my cellar. I'm so glad you're going to be helping Andie and me out getting this place back to looking good again! What do you say to all this Andie?" Maggie asked to make her feel included.

"He looks to be a lot stronger than we are, Maggie, I say his muscles could come in mighty handy." Andie held out her hand and shook Silas's hand. "Welcome aboard!"

Silas was floored. In the space of a few minutes, he was given a job, the hopes of clean clothes, good food and acceptance. It was a lot more than he ever thought he'd have today.

Maggie and Andie hurried to change clothes out of the pants and shirt. Maggie grabbed the money that she had inherited from Stephen's winning poker hand and they walked out the door with Silas toward the resale shop.

True to her word, Maggie made Silas pick out several pairs of pants, shirts, long john's, socks, shoes, jacket, hat and suspenders. While she was there, she asked Grace about the pile of rugs she had in the corner of her shop.

"Someone brought those in. I've washed them up, but there doesn't seem to be much value in rag rugs these days, I'll probably have to throw them out. Why do you ask?" Grace was a little puzzled over Maggie showing up with a black man and buying him clothes out of the blue. It wasn't like something that Maggie would do.

"How many rugs are there?" Maggie asked, almost afraid to breathe.

"I'd say about twelve or so. They're different sizes, but still usable."

"I'll take them off your hands if you want. I'll even give you fifty cents for the entire bundle. What do you say?" Maggie asked her.

"Sold! I'm thrilled to get rid of them. Is there anything else I can help you with today?" Grace quickly added up the total for all the clothes and the rugs.

"No, thanks, the clothes and the rugs really helped me out. Oh, by the way this is my new hired hand, Silas. If I send him up for something, feel free to send it back with him." Silas tipped his head to the lady at the cash register and picked up the large bundle of rugs. Andie picked up the bundle of his clothes and shoes and grinned up at the little black man. Maggie led the way out the door.

"Silas, I know those rugs are heavy. Why don't you take them back to the house? Andie and I are going to order some lumber to be delivered to the house today. You might want to clear a place to put about two wagons of planks and 2"x 4" s. We'll also pick up some nails. We'll meet you back at the house. By the way, my name is Maggie McDonald. I expect you to call me Maggie like everyone else. We'll come up with a last name for you to adopt. Everyone needs two names, a first and a last. Is there a person you really liked or admired, Silas?"

"Well, I liked that Lincoln fellow that got himself killed. I like the Washington gent who was President a long time ago...Could I use either of their names?" Silas asked.

"Of course! Which do you prefer?" Maggie asked him with a smile.

"I don't rightly know, how about the little girl decides." Silas sent a beseeching look towards Andie.

"I like the sound of Silas Washington." Andie told them proudly. They all nodded, Silas Washington was his new name!

While Silas carried the rugs back home, Andie and Maggie went and ordered and paid for lumber to be delivered to her house by noon. They stopped at the cooper smith and ordered several smaller barrels, buckets and the largest barrel they had. They told Maggie they would deliver them all sometime this morning. Then Maggie headed toward the General Store. She had some trading to do.

Jonah greeted her as they entered the store and asked what he could help her with today.

Maggie smiled, "Jonah, are you still interested in buying a real bath tub for Olivia?"

"Why, Maggie, you know that Liv has had her heart set on having a real bath tub ever since we got here. But they're way too expensive. Why do you ask?" Jonah was puzzled at her question.

"Well, I have a claw footed bath tub that I will trade to you, if you're of a mind to get the tub." Maggie waited on his answer.

"I'd love to surprise her with the tub, what are you asking for it?"

"I would like to trade the tub for a dozen chickens, a rooster, a young pig, a milking cow and a roll of chicken fencing. Do you think that would be a fair trade?"

"I'll do it! Those tubs are expensive and to get it shipped all the way out here...are you sure you want to get rid of it?" Jonah was excited. His anniversary was coming up and he would love to see his wife's face when he presented her with a real bath tub!

"I'd consider it a bargain, Jonah! Now I do need to buy a box of nails, a small hammer and some chicken feed!" Maggie laughed and squeezed Andie's hand. "Andie, it looks like you're going to get fresh milk, butter and eggs every day if you want them. Will you mind helping me take care of the animals?"

"Really!!?? You'd let me help gather eggs and everything? I will love it!" Andie told her hugging her. Life at the new boarding house just kept getting better and better.

"Oh, Jonah, you'd better add a butter churn to my list." Maggie thought a while and then asked him, "I know that Mary Murphy has been making you dresses each week to sell. She's pretty far along with her pregnancy, is she still sewing for you?"

"We gave her material to make us some dresses last fall, but when I went to pick them up, she had them done but told me with the baby and all, she didn't know if she'd have the time to continue to sew for us. I'm still going to stop by each week and pick up her extra butter and eggs and drop off whatever she's of a mind to trade for. We'll sure miss having her sew for us. Why do you ask?" Jonah asked her in return.

"My sister and brother-in-law just sent me a sewing machine. As long as I wouldn't be taking anything away from Mary, I think I could sew you some dresses each week and I might have some extra eggs and butter to trade with you, too..." Maggie's voice kind of faded away. She didn't want to put Jonah in a tight spot with asking about doing the sewing, but the money was just too good to pass up. With the meat the Sheriff and Deputy were going to supply and the vegetables from her garden, plus the eggs from the chickens and the milk and butter from the cow, she might even be able to put a little money aside to save or even to trade for the items she needed.

Jonah's answer was to yell for Olivia to come over, he had something important to tell her. "Liv guess what, we've got us another seamstress who's going to make us some dresses like Mary was doing! Maggie said she just got a sewing machine and she said she'd like to have a go at it. Go pick out some patterns and material so she can take it home with her. I'll get the rest of her order and

I'll be bringing the rest of your 'trade' over this afternoon and pick up that item you mentioned. Is that all right with you, Maggie?"

"It would be perfect, Jonah. Would you deliver the chicken feed at the same time, that way Andie and I won't have to carry it all the way home? Is Josie around, I'd like to introduce her to Andie. I think they're about the same age." Josie was the Clark's daughter; they also had a son, Oliver, who was about twelve.

"She's at the Murray's visiting with Bessie, their daughter. But I'll send her over as soon as she gets home, how will that be?" Liv told her as she picked out material, thread and patterns. "I'm so excited that we'll still be getting some dresses to sell. They go like hotcakes! I can't keep them in the store!" She gave the package to Maggie and gave her a hug as well.

Jonah finished the rest of her order and gave her the box to carry everything home. With all the nails, it was heavy. Maggie knew that she would sure be glad to get it home! She was thrilled with the trade she had made with Jonah. She had to use precious little of her money to get them the animals she wanted to raise. Now she just had to see how good Silas was at fixing them all up with pens! It promised to be a very busy afternoon!

CHAPTER 6

Silas was even better than he told her much to Maggie's delight! He had put the rugs on her back porch and then started cleaning out the barn. He not only swept out all the old straw, he literally scrubbed out the loft and cleaned out the stalls, so they looked like new! He knocked down spider webs and using the boards from her crated up sewing machine, he shored up several of the stalls as well. Maggie couldn't believe all he had gotten done in the time she ordered lumber and stopped in at the General Store.

"Silas, you are a miracle worker! I can't believe all you've gotten done in such a short space of time. In a very short time, our lumber, barrels, buckets and livestock will be arriving." At his look of surprise, Maggie continued, "We've got chickens and a rooster coming, a small pig and a milking cow. Andie and I will help you build a chicken coup, a small pen for the pig and a corral of some sort that the cow can graze in. Also, I've got a really large half barrel that we're going to use for a bath tub in the corner of the kitchen. Do you think that you could fix it so all we have to do is pull the plug and the water from the tub will drain into our garden? It would be so much easier than having to empty out bucket after bucket of water each night!"

"Why sure Miz Maggie, that shouldn't be no problem at all. Do you want me to fix myself a place up in the loft to sleep? It won't take no time at all to see it done..." Silas asked her.

"No, Silas, you're going to be staying in the house. I'm getting rid of the bath tub and the bathing room, that's going to be your room. I've got a cot and Andie and I will make up your bed with some sheets and warm blankets and a quilt. There's a small window that I'll wash and put a curtain up over it and I want to use one of those rugs you carried home today to lay in front of the cot, so your feet won't hit the cold floor first thing in the morning. I thought we'd put some nails in the wall to hang up your clothes. It'll be small, but cozy. And I know you'll be warm this winter being so close to the cook stove. How does that sound to you?" Maggie was excited; she thought she had come up with a place for him to sleep without too many problems.

"Miz Maggie, you want me to stay in the same house as all you white people are living? You don't have to go to all that trouble...I'll be fine in the barn." Silas told her, his mind reeling from having the chance to actually sleep in a real house.

"You'll do no such thing! The barn is cold and drafty. You'll stay in the house just like everybody else. And since I'm your boss, there'll be no discussion. Is that all right with you, Silas?" She saw him nod his head, his eyes big as saucers, "And another thing, we eat our meals in the kitchen. That's where I'll expect you to eat too, with us. Do we understand each other? We're in this together, you, Andie and me. We will work together, sleep in the same house and we will eat together, too. Now if you'll excuse us, Andie and I have to change our clothes. We'll be out to help you shortly."

Silas stood and watched them walk into the house. It had been his lucky day to get caught in Miz Maggie's barn. He suddenly smiled as he went back to work.

Lumber was delivered, barrels were delivered and so was all the livestock. As soon as the lumber arrived, Silas started on the chicken coup. Andie and Maggie helped him stretch the chicken wire all around the pen and across the top as well. He fixed them up a place in the barn and outside, so they could enjoy the fresh air. He made them a small container to hold their water and their chicken feed. He used the last of the crate wood and the crates they

39

came in to make them boxes to nest in and lay their eggs. They turned the chickens loose and watched them strut all around their enclosure. Andie loved watching them peck at the ground. Maggie promised to send out all her potato peels and her carrot peelings to feed to the chickens. Next on the agenda was the pig pen.

Silas hammered in several 2" by 4"s that had been cut into three pieces. Then he stretched the chicken wire around the wood. The pig pen didn't take near as long to make as the chicken coup. Andie had the honors of carrying the pig and letting it go. She quickly named the pig, Porky. Silas cut a small barrel length wise and made a watering trough and a feeding trough.

They had let the cow wander around munching on the tall grass. Silas said he'd see about building a corral tomorrow, in the meantime, they'd stake out the cow so she could keep eating. Maggie and Andie headed back into the house to get Silas's room ready. Jonah had already picked up the long tub. Maggie started scrubbing the floor and the walls. She let Andie hammer in the nails to hang up Silas's clothes. She carried down the cot she kept in the upstairs closet for any of her boarders who might have had someone spending the night. They put on sheets, blankets and a colorful quilt that Andie liked. It didn't take any time at all to sew up some curtains for the small window. Maggie put one of the rugs down by the cot and they were done.

She and Andie rolled the extra-large half barrel into the corner of the kitchen. They hammered in a blanket to give them some privacy and put in a small table that Maggie used to have in the bathing chamber for towels and the lantern. In the next day or so, they hoped that Silas would fix it up to drain into the garden they were going to put in.

Maggie and Andie then started cutting up the meat and vegetables from last night's meal, making it into beef stew. She let Andie mix up the biscuits and helped her put them in the oven.

They set the table for five, making sure that they had room for Silas at the table with them. Maggie didn't even worry about Sam and Reece accepting Silas at her table, she hoped they would accept him as she and Andie had.

Then she had Andie help her make up a quick peach cobbler with the left over biscuit dough and dinner was ready to go. She and Andie both went and changed back into their skirts to eat dinner with. They were both feeling good about the changes they had set in motion today. They just had to wait for Sam and Reece to come home. Maggie wondered if they had been able to get any game while they visited the ranches in the area and if they had given her message to the Murphy's.

Sam and Reece were heading back to town after riding out to meet as many farmers and ranchers as they could. Sam liked the hard-working men and women who were making a go of it in a hard land. He was impressed with the Murphy's. They had a real nice spread and from the sound of it, Mary was the cause of most of it. She was really pregnant, but still managed to invite them to lunch with all of them. She gave them some vegetable beef soup and a ham sandwich that sure tasted good. Her cabin was spotless even with five children running around. The first thing she asked about was Maggie. She was worried about her. They hadn't been able to see much of each other over the winter and she hoped she'd gotten along all right.

Sam put her mind at ease, telling her that she looked good and her house was amazing. She had made them feel welcome and that she and his niece got along like a house afire. She was going to look after Andie and he and Reece were going to try and fill up her smokehouse for her.

Mary laughed, "That sounds just like a deal that Maggie would make! She always got along really well with my kids. She's a favorite of theirs."

"She sounded real partial to your kids, too. She asked me to ask your older boys if they would have time to bring her in a couple wagon loads of cut wood when they had the time and also if they could bring the plow to dig up her garden. She said that your canned vegetables and smoked meat got her through the winter and now she's going to make a big garden with Andie's help to help feed us all this summer and winter. As good as the dinner was last night, I won't mind that at all. Reece and I will do our part that's for sure."

The boys were excited about being able to help out Maggie again and talked to Cade about when would be a good time to borrow the plow.

"I'm almost done with plowing the fields and planting. There will be a few days where I'm planting before I'll need you to start helping with the cattle. Why don't you plan on helping out Maggie the beginning of next week? You should have several days to chop wood and then take several loads in to her. Sheriff, why don't you tell Maggie the wood and the plow will be there the first of next week." Cade told them.

"Also ask Maggie if she wants to come out and help me pick berries when they're ripe," Mary added. "Cade won't let me pick them by myself; he's worried about me and the baby. So, I could really use her help!"

"She wondered if I'd mind if she brought Andie out with her to pick berries, so I'm thinking she's planning on coming out anyway. Is there a certain day you want them to come?" Sam asked.

"Let's see...today's Wednesday, see if Friday works for her, if not we'll make it early next week." Mary told him.

"I'll be sure to tell her, we thank you for the invite to lunch. It was sure delicious. Mrs. Murphy, you're sure a good cook. If you have any problems, send word, we'll be out as soon as we can. You'll be seeing us on our patrols about twice a week. You folks take care..." Both Sam and Reece waved good bye to the family and headed for home. They had chosen not to shoot anything until they were headed for home because they didn't want to cart around dead animals while they met all the new folks. Now they took the time to find some meat for Maggie.

Luck was with them, they each got a deer and a turkey and Reece was able to get off a couple of good shots at some wild hens. He was able to get three before they scattered. They field dressed the animals and then headed back to town. It had been a long and productive day. Reece wondered what they were having for dinner! He was starved even after the sandwiches Maggie had sent with them and the lunch Mrs. Murphy had given them. They were not prepared for all the changes they saw as they brought the game to the smokehouse.

The smokehouse was clean and ready for any and all the meat they had brought. But there was a chicken coup and a pig pen and was that a cow? They also noticed a little black man working on building a corral. He looked to be right handy with a hammer and nails! They couldn't wait to go into dinner and find out what was going on!

About that same time, Andie comes running out of the house yelling, "Uncle Sam! Uncle Sam, guess what we did today?!" He couldn't believe how happy she looked; she was almost giddy with joy. Sam's heart filled with love for his niece and for the woman who had erased the gloom that had found a home in Andie's soul.

"I give up pumpkin, but it sure looks different around here now than when Reece and I left this morning. Somebody's been busy..." Sam told her with a chuckle.

"Silas is our new handy man! He helped us build a chicken coup and a pig pen and he's making a clean stall for our cow! Maggie and me helped him and we also cleaned out her smoke house and her bathing room. That's where Silas is going to live now. Maggie

43

traded her big bath tub for a different tub and all the animals. Now we're going to have milk and eggs and butter all the time to help me grow big and strong. And guess what?" Andie ran out of air and paused.

"What?" Sam told her with a smile.

"Maggie said I get to help her feed the chickens and the pig and even gather eggs. She already found a basket for me to put the eggs in! I also helped make dinner with Maggie. I made the biscuits and helped with the peach cobbler. Did we surprise you?!"

"You sure did! Will you run tell Maggie that Reece and I are back, and we have a lot of meat to put in the smoke house? How long do we have before dinner will be ready?" Sam told her even while helping Reece take the animals, they had tied onto the backs of the horses off. He wasn't looking forward to skinning and cutting up all the meat they had found. But he knew it had to be done and done quickly so they wouldn't lose any of it.

Andie was off like a shot and ran into the kitchen slamming the door behind her. Reece smiled at her excitement, "I think that Andie is starting to feel at home around here. I kind of like the idea of being able to have butter and eggs a lot. And the milk will sure be good for Andie." He told Sam and then looked up as a little grey-haired black man ambled over to where they were standing.

"My name is Silas...Washington. Miz Maggie hired me to work around here for her today. You gents need some help skinning and cutting up that meat to put into the smokehouse? If you do, I'm your man. I been skinning animals and cutting them up to put into smokehouses all my life..." With that he took out a knife he had in his back pocket and proceeded to skin the deer. He had no wasted movement and before long had the entire skin off and ready to nail to the barn wall. He told Sam to get a pot of boiling water to dip the turkeys and hens in; it would make it easier to take off the feathers.

About that same time, Maggie came out of the house carrying some rather wicked looking knives.

"Wow, you men outdid yourselves getting us game for the smokehouse! Thank you very much!" Then she turned to Silas, "I have some bigger knives for you to use, Silas, they should make cutting up the deer meat easier. I already put on a pot of water to dip the feathered meat in. I'll bring it out when it's hot enough. Dinner will be ready when you men are." With that, Maggie turned around and headed back to the house.

Silas then proceeded to show them how to cut up the venison. By the time he was done, Maggie came out carrying the big pot of boiling water for them. By dipping the birds into the water, their feathers seemed to almost fall off of them. Maggie had even given them a pillow case to put the feathers in. She told them she used them to make their pillows with. With all three of them working, it didn't take them long at all to get the meat skinned, cut and hung in the smokehouse. Andie brought them enough wood to start the fire under the meat and together they all headed to the house to clean up and eat dinner.

Sam and Reece both noted the blanket hanging in the corner of the room and looking behind it, they discovered the biggest half barrel they had ever seen. Maggie explained that she needed the bathing room for Silas, and she thought it would be easier to drill a hole in the barrel than in the porcelain bath tub. Silas was going to run a hose from the barrel into her garden, so they wouldn't have to empty out the tub after they bathed. Both men thought it was an excellent suggestion.

Silas hesitated to sit down with all the white people; he still hadn't come to terms with all that had happened to him today. Getting a job, getting some new clothes and even shoes, not having to sleep outside or to sneak into someone's barn and getting enough food to eat, it all seemed too good to be true.

"Silas, why don't you sit on my left Andie sits on my right and Sam and Reece will sit across from us. Everyone sit down, I'll dish out the beef stew and Andie will pass out the biscuits. I should add that she made them herself and they are light as a feather. There's peach cobbler for dessert. I thought we needed to celebrate a clean smoke house and meat to go in it! Then there are the new additions of chickens, a pig and a cow and most importantly adding a new member to our household, Silas. The man can sure do just about anything. Let's pray and then you can all dig in. We made a lot for our hungry men, didn't we Andie?" Maggie sat down and grabbed Andie's hand and Silas's, everyone else did the same. "Bless us our Lord for all our blessings that you have seen fit to give to us. We don't take lightly how good you've been to us with the meat, chickens, pig, cow and Silas. Thank you for all these blessings, Amen!" When she looked up it was to see a very tender look on Sam's face as he gazed at the picture, she made holding hands with his niece and a black man. Maggie McDonald was sure some woman!

CHAPTER 7

It was while they were eating the dinner, she and Andie had prepared that Maggie brought up the idea of using their barn to stable Reece and Sam's horses.

"Silas has the barn looking and smelling really good. We have some extra stalls if you men would like to stable your horses in our barn instead of the livery." Maggie paused letting the idea sink in and then continued. "I don't think that Silas would mind taking care of your horses and it sure would be more convenient when you have to grab your horses and go after someone." She paused again, "I think the going rate for a month at the livery is about seven dollars for each of your horses. I think if you each paid four dollars each, Silas would get three of the four dollars and the other dollar would go toward bringing in a load of straw or hay and the bags of oats we would buy. I'm only giving Silas room and board; this way he would be getting some cash to spend the way he would like. How does that sound to you gentlemen?"

Silas couldn't believe his ears! He was actually going to get paid for helping out these kind people. His life kept getting better and better!

"I like the idea of keeping the horses here, Maggie, as long as Silas doesn't mind the extra work the horses would be. I also like the idea of saving money each month." Sam was the first to respond.

"It sure would be convenient. If Silas is as good with horses as he was at cutting and skinning the game we brought in, he should be pretty good in the stable, too. I say we do it, because like you said, we would be saving money. Saving three dollars over the course of a year means we'll save over thirty-five dollars. How do you feel about the extra work, Silas?" Reece asked him.

They were asking him and not telling him that he would be taking care of the horses. "I would gladly take care of your horses...the corral will be done tomorrow. The horses will be eating fresh grass every day outside, which is better than being in a stall all the time. I could sure use the money that's for sure, although Miz Maggie has sure given me the world already with clothes, food and a good place to stay."

"Then consider it done." Sam announced to the table at large but smiled at Silas. "Reece and I will get the horses after dinner and bring them home. We'll pay you for the month when we come. Who are you going to ask to bring in the load of hay, Maggie?"

"Mitch Drew. He and his family live out near Cade and Mary Murphy. He delivers loads of straw to the livery; I think he'd be glad to bring us a load every month. We can get the oats from the General Store tomorrow. I'll ask Jonah to ask Mitch or Ava when they come in to get their spring supplies if we don't see them in the next few days." She looked up and smiled at Silas. He was beaming at his new status and station in life. It was a lot different than when he woke up this morning!

"Sounds good. That was sure a good meal Maggie and Andie; I don't know when I've eaten such light biscuits! I sure hope you get to make them a lot! Reece, if you're done, let's go get our horses and gear and settle up with the livery and then settle up with Silas and Maggie. Andie, do you want to come with us?" Sam asked getting up out of his chair.

"Yeah, I would, Uncle Sam. Do you think they have any puppies or kittens at the livery?" Andie asked hopefully. She had always wanted her own cat or dog, but at the other boarding house they weren't allowed. She was sure that Maggie would let her keep them in the barn if not in the house.

"I don't know, honey, but we'll sure see when we get there. We'll be back as soon as we can. Thanks for the fine meal, Maggie and the lunch were really tasty, too." Sam tipped his hat and the three walked out the door.

"Miz Maggie, how am I ever going to be able to repay you for being so good to me?" Silas asked her in a quiet voice.

"Silas, you don't have to ever thank me! It's I who should be thanking you! I have wanted for a long time to get chickens and a cow and to have someone who knows how to make things to make everything so much better around here for all of us. You will make that possible! You'll probably want me to stop coming up with projects real soon, so you won't have to work so hard! Your coming when you did was a blessing. Thank you for everything you're doing and willing to do to help me out!" Maggie stretched out her hand and grabbed hold of Silas's hand. "We are a team, you and me. I hate being lonely and with you and my boarders, I feel doubly blessed." Silas just nodded his head, he had never had a white woman be so kind to him or had one touch him in kindness. He was humbled by her goodness and vowed to be the best worker he could be for her.

Maggie got up and started to do the dishes. She hummed while she worked. Silas went out to milk the cow and settle the animals down for the night. He also wanted to make sure he had two stalls clean and ready for when the Sheriff and his Deputy came back.

They were back before you knew it and Andie was grinning from ear to ear. She was holding a wiggling bundle in her arms. When Sam lifted her down from his saddle, she ran to Maggie and showed her what she was holding. It was a puppy! He was adorable and Maggie fell in love with it as soon as she saw it.

49

"Maggie, can we keep him? I promise to feed him and keep him out of trouble...I always wanted a dog..." Andie's voice got softer.

"Well, of course, we can keep him as long as your Uncle and Silas agree." Maggie told her hugging Andie and the squirming bundle. "I think having a dog would be good for all of us. He can act as a watch dog and you can play with him. I would prefer to him sleeping in the barn instead of your room. Is that all right Andie?"

"I love you Maggie!" Andie told him. "Uncle Sam, can I keep him? Do you mind Silas? I promise not to make any more work for you to do?"

Silas and Sam looked at each other and they both started laughing. "When, I let her take him home, I told her that if Maggie said it was all right, it was all right with me. Andie, it looks like Silas, Maggie and I are all right with you getting a puppy!" Sam told her leading his horse to the barn with Reece. "What are you going to call him?"

The puppy had already gone to the bathroom twice just in the short time he had been there. "Maybe you should call him Puddles!" Reece told her in jest.

"How about...Paddy?" Andie suggested. "He needs to have a first and a last name...we'll call him Paddy Puddles!"

"Paddy it is Andie. What kind of puppy is he?" Maggie liked petting the soft dark brown hair and having him lick her fingers.

"He's probably part collie and part shepherd and part mutt!" Sam told her stopping to pet the bundle of fur. "Let's go make a bed for him in the barn."

"Why don't you take one of the rugs we got today at the resell shop? Put him in one of the stalls we have and that will keep him safe until morning and then you can give him a bath to get rid of any fleas. How does that sound, Andie?" Maggie suggested.

"Should I sleep in the barn with him? He'll probably get lonely without anyone out there with him..." She looked up at her Uncle Sam waiting for him to let her.

"Nope, not this time Andie. You will sleep in your own bed. The sooner Paddy gets used to where he's supposed to sleep, the sooner it'll be better for all of us. You can play with him as much as you want to tomorrow. Grab one of those rugs, Maggie mentioned and let's get him settled." Sam told her gently.

"I'll bring him out some milk Andie. He'll eat and fall asleep and probably won't wake up until you wake up tomorrow. We'll get even more milk tomorrow and maybe some toast."

Andie smiled, so happy she had her own dog, she would have agreed to just about anything! Sam carried Paddy, Andie grabbed a small rag rug and Maggie went into get a small bowl of milk to the newest member of the family.

Silas put the two horses into stalls and made sure they had fresh water and a mound of freshly cut grass to feed them for the night. They'd get oats for them tomorrow and he would attempt to put up a lot of cut grass until they got the straw delivered. He also found them saw horses to put their saddles on and a shelf to hold their curry combs and picks to clean their horseshoes. Reece and Sam gave three dollars each to Silas and the last two dollars to Maggie to buy the straw and the oats. They got Paddy settled for the night and they all went into the house.

Maggie insisted that Silas take a bath before he got into his nice clean sheets and blankets. She wanted to be able to wash out his dirty clothes in the morning with all the other clothes from the rest of the group. Maggie felt like they were almost a family. She liked how everybody got along and how comfortable she was beginning to feel with Sam and Reece. Andie had gotten under her skin so quickly; she was already in love with her. For the first time, Maggie almost felt like she was her mother. She loved having her with her most of the day and teaching the things that she would have been teaching her own children if she had ever been blessed with her own babies. Maggie was happier than she had been in many years. For the first time in a long, long time, Maggie found herself to be content. It was a good feeling.

CHAPTER 8

Silas loved sleeping in a real bed even if it was only a cot! For the first time that he could remember, he was clean, warm and had a full stomach! He dressed in some of his clean clothes and put on his new boots. The feeling of wearing socks and shoes was a unique one for Silas. He hadn't been able to afford to have either for quite some time; he had been worried about what to do when it started to get colder. He immediately went out to the barn and milked the cow, gathered the eggs and gave some fresh warm milk to Paddy. He then hobbled the cow and both horses in the tall long grass behind the barn. He'd move them to the corral as soon as he finished with building it. Then he wanted to run hoses from the new tub and the kitchen sink out to Maggie's garden or at least to where it will be. He knew he'd need to make a trip to the General Store to get oats and the hose. He also couldn't wait to make Maggie's cellar. It was sure good to feel needed and to have so many jobs to choose from. He was a lucky man!

Maggie took the eggs and the milk and started making breakfast. She strained the milk and the cream just like she had done last night and hoped she'd have enough to churn butter this morning. She made pancakes and ham for breakfast and started a batch of bread. She made sandwiches with the last of her bread from yesterday for Reece and Sam to take with them. She started making a mental note of all she needed to get done today. She'd go with Silas to get the oats and to talk with Jonah about the Drew's getting them a load of straw. Then she needed to wash clothes and start sewing on the five dresses that she needed to make for the Clark's.

By the time that Maggie had the pancakes done, Sam, Reece, Silas and Andie were down and ready for breakfast. They loved the pancakes and Andie was out the door as soon as she was done to go see Paddy. She even carried a pancake to feed to him for his own breakfast. Silas headed outside to work on the corral until Maggie was ready to go to the store. Reece and Sam headed off with the sandwiches for the jail and to begin their rounds. It was a good morning for all of them.

Maggie made beds and picked up all the dirty clothes and heated up water to wash all the clothes on the porch. It was a lot easier to wash clothes outside than inside and the porch was high enough to make it easier on her back. Sam had told her that the Murphy boys would be here on Monday with wood and a plow. She also planned to go berry picking on Friday, if they hadn't seen the Drew's by then, Maggie would stop and order the straw for the barn. It was midmorning by the time they were all free to head to the store. Silas had tied a rope around the neck of Paddy and gave the rest of the rope to Andie to hold so that Paddy wouldn't run out into the middle of the street and get hurt by all the wagons traveling up and down the road.

At the General Store, they bought the oats and enough hose to run to the garden for both the sink and the tub. Maggie was thrilled at the thought of not having to empty the tub again and to be able to just throw the used water down her sink instead of carrying it outside every time she did washing.

Josie Clark came over carrying a small kitten. Andie loved the kitten and they were both soon playing with the kitten on the kitchen floor with a string of yarn. Andie loved having someone to play with and Silas took out time to make them a swing in the backyard. Andie gave him a hug and they took turns playing with the puppy, the kitten and swinging each other in the swing. Josie had to go home by noon, but they decided to see each other the next day as long as it was all right with Olivia, Josie's mother.

Silas finished the corral and turned each of the animals free inside the enclosure. It was built very sturdy and was a welcome addition. Then he went to work on digging a trench from the house to the garden. He was going to use the same trench for both the sink and the tub, they would start at different places in the kitchen, but by the time he joined them in the back of the house, he would only have to dig one trench to the garden. It didn't take him long at all to bore a hole for the tub and the wall and from the sink through the wall. He spent the rest of the afternoon digging the trench to the garden. When he was done and it was covered, he let Andie throw the first bowl of water down the sink and come out in the garden.

Maggie had indeed made butter and been able to start on the skirts for all five dresses. She had the bodices on two of the dresses done and just had to attach them to the skirt. The Singer sewing machine was much faster than sewing by hand. Maggie loved how easy it was to make the dresses. She still had time to feed lunch to Silas, Andie and herself and make up a vegetable beef soup for dinner. She set a large pan of beans to soaking thinking to make ham and beans tomorrow night for dinner and then had time for making up a cake for dessert. Andie helped make the icing for the cake.

Andie was having the time of her life! She had loved having a friend and a puppy and a kitten to play with. She ran in and out of the house countless times during the day and didn't have to worry once about getting yelled at for slamming the door or wiping her feet. She knew that Maggie liked her and didn't mind her chatter or her activities.

Sam and Reece didn't have to ride out to the Drew's place to order a load of straw; Mitch Drew came into town looking for them.

"Sheriff, I hate to bother you so soon after you came to town, but I'm losing some cattle. My boy and I've searched all over and can't find them. I can't afford to lose any of my cattle; if its cattle rustling, I want those cattle back before they get taken up to Cheyenne and sold. I've not got a chance to talk to any of my neighbors to see if they're missing any, but it's probably a good chance. We all check on our cattle a lot, but in the spring we're so busy plowing and planting, we don't watch them as we should. There are only so many hours in a day. If you wouldn't mind checking it out, I sure would appreciate it." Mitch told him.

"My deputy and I will get our horses and ride out with you, Mr. Drew. You can show us where you keep your cattle and we'll nose around and see what we can see. While you're here, my landlady, Maggie McDonald, says that you sell straw and hay. We need to get a load to help fill the barn at her house. We'll probably need you to bring us a load every month or so. Will that be a problem?" Sam asked him as they walked the short distance to Maggie's boarding house.

"I'd be glad of the opportunity to sell some of it, Sheriff. I didn't know Maggie had opened up the barn at her place. She's a real nice lady, who's had a heap of trouble keeping body and soul together the last few years. She was married to a no-account gambler. Maggie threw him out of her bedroom when she found out he was cheating on her. I heard that she made him pay rent just like all her other boarder's after that. I only ran into him a couple of times, but he was always trying to talk someone out of something or other. He wasn't worth the powder it would take to blow him away. Cade Murphy has known her since the time they were little kids, and he threatened to beat the shit out of him more than once if he didn't treat Maggie better. Don't know if it would have done any good, but it sure would have made Cade feel better. I'll bring up a load of straw later today for you." Mitch told him.

Sam didn't want to listen to any gossip about Maggie, but he found himself interested in spite of himself to learn more about Maggie. She intrigued him. She was sure an independentwoman, used to doing things for herself. But you also could tell she was lonely. She seemed to light up whenever Andie was around, and she also seemed to like the company of Reece, Silas and himself. He sure found that he smiled a lot more when he was around her. She was a pretty lady, still young enough to marry again and have plenty of young'uns' to help keep her company. The thought of Maggie being with another man didn't set too well with Sam. He wasn't sure why, but the thought of being with Maggie brightened his day. The thought of her being with someone else made him feel troubled. He wanted her happy; she deserved to be after all she'd been through. He just didn't know how to go about helping her reach her happiness.

They found Silas digging a trench to drain the water from the tub and the sink in the backyard. "Silas, Reece and I are going to head out to Mitch Drew's place to look around for some cattle rustlers. I don't know when we'll be back, so tell Maggie not to hold supper on account of us. Also, Mitch is going to bring in a load of straw this afternoon. Everything going all right?" Sam asked the little man.

"I'll let Miz Maggie know about the straw and the late supper for you all. You be careful now and don't worry about anything around here. I'll watch out for Miz Andie and Miz Maggie." Silas told him solemnly. "Let me help you get your horses. They're in the corral, I finished it this morning. They sure do seem to like grazing on that lush green grass."

Silas caught the two horses and handed them over to Reece and Sam. He waved to the three gentlemen and headed to the house to tell Maggie they wouldn't be in for dinner and that the straw would be delivered this afternoon.

57

Andie came running out of the house holding a kitten in her arms. "Uncle Sam! Uncle Sam! Look what Josie gave me this morning!!" She was grinning from ear to ear.

"Did you ask Maggie about keeping a kitten on top of a new puppy?" Sam reached down to pet the tiny bundle of fur.

"She likes cats and gave me some yarn to play with. I've decided to call her Minerva Kitty...but Minnie for short. What do you think...do you like her?"

"Yes, pumpkin, I do. But she's the last pet you're going to ask for, all right? You're going to be busy keeping them all fed and clean and out of Maggie's hair! We'll be late coming home. You make sure that Minnie beds down with Paddy in the barn, all right?" Sam asked her as he started to ride out.

"Thanks, Uncle Sam! I promise to bed her down with Paddy!" Andie called out to him as he left. Then she went back to playing with Paddy and Minnie.

Being able to sew all day, Maggie made a big dent in the making of the five dresses. She only had the hand work to do and she'd be able to take them to Jonah at the General Store. In the back of her mind was her wish list and she was getting all she had wished for right and left these last few days! She knew that Jonah had worked out a deal where Mary and Cade got three horses up front and then Mary made dresses, butter, soap and gave him eggs for about six weeks afterwards. Maggie wondered if he'd do the same for her. Every time she went out to Mary's, she had to rent a buggy and a horse. I wonder how much a buggy and a horse cost. I know we have room in the barn for another horse and there's room to park the buggy in the back of the barn. It would sure be nice to have the buggy to drive to the General Store to pick up supplies instead of having to carry it all home in her arms. She'd sew all summer for a chance to have her own buggy and horse! She made a mental note to aske Jonah tomorrow when she brought the five dresses, extra eggs and extra butter in. She was excited all over again!

Meanwhile, Reece and Sam were following tracks of the cattle that were stolen. They were able to find where they were taken and several others as well, but they didn't find the rustlers. They helped return the cattle to Mr. Drew and to the Grahams and a few were Cade Murphy's. Reece and Sam were disappointed at not getting the rustlers, but at least they didn't lose any cattle. They promised to check back with them often to make sure they didn't take them again.

They rode back to town hot, dusty and tired. One of Maggie's delicious meals sounded good, along with a hot bath, seemed like a perfect evening. This would probably be the last time they would be working together. Starting tomorrow, they would have two different shifts. Sam would start early in the morning and work till dinner time around 6:00 p.m. Reece would start around noon and work until midnight. They didn't feel the need to have both working the same hours. This way they would have someone working from 6:00 a.m. until midnight. Unless they ran into trouble, they would try out the new schedule for a few weeks and see how it worked. Reece wanted them both to make their presence known in the saloons. He wanted to clear out the trigger hungry men and make Pine City a clean, safe place to live and raise their families in. Sam was content to let things ride until there was trouble. Then, they would shut them down and clean them out.

This was the first Saturday night in Pine City, so far it was a quiet night. They planned to have a quiet supper and then make rounds to keep the rowdies controlled. It didn't quite work out that way.

First, they had to arrest two cowboys for being drunk and disorderly as soon as they got back into town. They had no sooner locked them up, when there was a shooting in one of the saloons over someone cheating over a card game. The doc was called, and the injured man was taken to his offices to get patched up. They confiscated the rest of the guns in the saloon, told them to pick them up from the jail as they left town, then they locked up the shooter in the card game. Sam didn't know many of the men in the saloon, but there were two sitting in the back of the saloon that rubbed Sam the wrong way. They seemed to be almost mocking him. As far as Sam knew, he had never met the men before. Who were they and what were they mocking? They were questions that Sam would find the answers to sooner or later.

A surprise was waiting for them when they came back to the office. Maggie had sent Silas and Andie over with a kettle of soup and sandwiches to eat while they were still hot. Did it ever hit the spot! Nobody had ever taken such good care of them before; Pine City was looking better and better to both Reece and Sam. Sam knew that Andie had never been happier, so he knew he had made a good decision in coming here. Silas looked like a different man all cleaned up and in clothes that fit him. He was sure proud of his new shoes and haircut. Silas told them he'd take the horses back to the barn and get them settled for the night, he'd be back later for the kettle and the bowls.

Andie told him all about her day with Josie, Minnie, Paddy and Maggie. She was filthy from playing outside all day with the puppy and the kitten, but she was smiling and chattering a mile a minute about how much fun it was living at Maggie's house. Sam was grateful to Maggie for making it such a great place for his niece to live. He'd have to be sure to thank her for the dinner and all her help in taking care of Andie. They were in a good situation that was for sure!

CHAPTER 9

Sunday was a clear day. Not much was going on in town, most of the businesses were closed on Sunday and the saloons didn't open until much later in the day. Silas decided to go down the stairs and check out Maggie's basement/cellar. Maggie was worried. She warned him there were snakes down there and she didn't want him to get bit. Silas hadn't taken but three steps down the stairs when he heard the shake of a rattlesnake's tail, possibly more than one. He hightailed it back up the stairs and told Maggie he needed to see Sam and Reece about clearing out the snakes, so he could start work on her cellar.

Sam and Reece were both at the jail feeding their prisoners. When Silas told them of the snakes, they both followed him home to help. Maggie had lit several lanterns, so they could see. She was almost in tears, she wanted her cellar but not at the cost of someone getting snake bit!

Each of the three men took a lantern and started down the stairs. They heard the rattles as soon as they cleared the doorway. Sam shot the first one he saw, but they still heard rattles. Reece shot another one and Silas pointed to another back by the wall. Sam shot that one. And then they waited for the sound of more rattles.

"Be careful, Sheriff, I hear they come in twos. You done shot three of them, there should be another one around here someplace..." Silas warned the two men.

They were able to climb down all the stairs and held the lanterns so that they could see in all the corners and along the walls. Silas almost stepped on the fourth one as he took a step off the stairs. It was curled up under the last step. Both Reece and Sam heard the rattles at the same time and they both shot the snake before it could bite Silas. Silas took a pitchfork to pick up the dead snakes and dispose of them. They could sure see why Maggie wanted a different place to store all her supplies and canned goods. They would also think twice before heading downstairs if a tornado came.

Since they were both there, they helped Silas with building the frame of the twelve feet by twelve feet room. It would completely encase the stairs and have four wooden walls, a wooden ceiling and a wooden floor. Maggie was determined to keep all snakes out of it!

It sure helped Silas to have extra hands while nailing up the frame. Andie and Maggie helped by dragging two by fours in and taking them to the cellar stairs. The men took what they needed and didn't have to go the barn to get them. It saved them a lot of time and Maggie and Andie liked helping. By the time they finished for the day, the frame was up, and the ceiling was in.

"Silas, every day until you get done, I want you check for snakes. They're getting in from someplace and until you make that room secure, there's always going to be the chance of a snake getting in. Do you have a gun?" Sam asked him.

"No...Sir, I don't got no gun. I never had enough money to buy me one." Silas told him.

"Come with me over to the jail, we've got some extra hand guns over there that I am going to give you. You go down in that cellar and you make sure that you're armed and ready to shoot. I'll take you back behind the barn tonight and have you practice loading and shooting. There's too much time that Reece or I will not be here, and I want Maggie and Andie protected. Do you feel alright using the gun?" Sam asked him.

"Yes, sir! I will protect the little ladies. I be careful, but I won't take no chances. I thank you for trusting me with their welfare." Silas puffed out his thin chest. He was proud that Sam was going to give him a gun. After all that Maggie had done for him, he'd make sure no harm befell her on his watch.

Maggie had put on ham and beans on the stove and they had simmered all day. She quickly made up cornbread to go with it. Andie set the table and her hungry men sat down to eat.

"Maggie I can't believe how many snakes you had downstairs! It was like a snake pit!" Reece told her taking another helping of the meal. "Some of those snakes were as big around as my arm! I can sure see why you didn't go downstairs!"

"When we first moved here ten years ago, they told us the house had a basement. We had basements back in Missouri where I grew up, but they always had concrete block walls. This was no basement! There's just dirt walls and a dirty, muddy floor. The first time I started to go down there, I saw two snakes. I refused to go back down. I'd take my chances on a tornado under my kitchen table. I always wanted to get a real cellar built, but I didn't have the money or the manpower. Now, that I do, I'm going to make it safe to store supplies down there and make it safe to go down in case of a tornado. We get a couple of scares from tornadoes every spring and summer. I will be so thankful for having a safe place to escape to! Sam, you and Reece make sure that if you see a tornado to come home and get in our cellar, too. It'll be plenty big enough for all of us to hide out until it's safe to get out." Maggie told all the men at the table to be safe rather than sorry!

"Will there be room for Paddy and Minnie?" Andie asked her as she buttered another square of cornbread.

"Of course, there will!" Maggie told her with a smile. "But not the horses, chickens, pig, or cow! They'll have to be content to stay in the barn."

They all laughed. It was a pleasant way to spend the evening on Maggie's front porch. You could sit on the swing or in one of her

63

benches. The men could smoke, and Andie could still play with her new pets. It was almost like they were a family.

Maggie brought up the possibility of buying a used buggy and horse. "I don't know anything about what to look for in getting a good deal. I can't pay much but it sure would make going out to Cade and Mary's easier and would also make getting supplies from the General Store easier. I must go daily to get everything I need, because I just can't carry that much with me at any one time. I also thought that if we got a mare to pull the buggy, we could mate her with your stallion, Sam and the colt would be just the right size for Andie someday to ride back and forth from school. What do you think?"

"My own pony! For real, Maggie, you are the best! Uncle Sam would that be all right with you? Please, please, pretty please say yes!" Andie cried out to Sam and begged. Her own horse, it would be a dream come true!

"It would sure complete the picture for you Andie, but let's not get the buggy before the horse! Reece and I will look over what's available at the livery. If we see something that would fit your needs, we'll tell you about it." Andie couldn't let Sam finish before she was jumping up and down in excitement. "But first we have to make sure that it's dependable. I don't want you buying a buggy and having it break down on the road somewhere between here and the Murphy's. Then we'll look at the horseflesh he's got. I don't want a horse that will go lame the first week we get her. Give Reece and me a day and we'll see what's available, agreed?"

Both Maggie and Andie nodded. They couldn't wait until tomorrow!

The Murphy boys, Cam and Chris, showed up bright and early, but they had brought along their little sister, Kit, to play with Andie. The wagon was filled high with cut wood. They had also remembered the plow. It was decided that one of them would plow the garden spot and one of them would unload and stack wood. Underneath the wood, were a layer of large rocks.

"What in the world, boys, is the rock for?" Asked an astonished Maggie.

"Ma said with all the boarders you have you don't need to be breaking your back washing out all the clothes. So, when Cam and I get done, we're going to build you a wash stand to wash your clothes on. Ma uses hers almost every day and she says it's great. Do you want one?" Chris asked her smiling.

"I'd love one, I've been using the porch, but this will be so much nicer! Thank you, boys and be sure to tell your mother thank you, too! Whatever will your mother think of next?" Maggie exclaimed.

"Our ma is smart, and she can build just about anything! Why when she came to us last year, she put in a wooden floor, cabinets, fixed the roof, chinked the walls of the cabin and the barn, made us all beds, helped us build chicken coups, pig pens and even showed pa how to make corn sheds to store our crops." Cam told her.

"Wait a minute, did you say your mother made your beds? Do you know how to do it?" Maggie interrupted them. Silas needed a real bed not a cot. If they could made him one, it would be wonderful.

"Why, we sure do. Ma showed us how and then we helped her make beds for all of us. It's not that hard. You need some planks, a couple of two by fours, some rope and a lot of nails. Do you got all that, Miz Maggie?"

"I'm pretty sure I do, if not, I'll go to the General Store to get it. I can't believe all that you're going to get done today, the garden, the wood pile, a wash stand, and Silas's bed. Thank you so much for all you've done for me, I really appreciate it!"

"No problem, now we'd best get started. Cam, you start unloading the wood and stacking it against the house. I'll take the plow and the mule and get that garden plowed. We'll pull some logs over it before we leave to break up the big clogs of dirt, then you should be ready to get your garden in. When both of those are done, we'll see about the wash stand and the bed. How does that sound?" Chris asked her already helping Cam to lift the plow from the wagon.

"Like music to my ears, I'll call you when lunch is ready. And if you need anything, just yell. Either Andie, Silas, or I will come running!" Maggie told the boys. "Kit I didn't even give you a hug and tell you how glad I am that you came out with the boys. Andie has some pets she can show you and a swing that Silas made for her yesterday. If you girls need anything, let me know." With that Maggie disappeared into the house. You could already hear the hammer of Silas in the cellar putting up the walls. Maggie took a deep breath at all she would be getting done today. It was a new day and a better outlook for her every day. On top of that, Reece and Sam were going to investigate getting her a buggy and a horse. She went into the house to get the dresses, butter and eggs to take to Jonah at the store and talk to him about paying for the buggy and horse. It was going to be a very busy morning!

Maggie had the two girls help her carry the butter and the eggs, while she carried the five dresses. They loved the dresses and sold two while she was standing there! "Jonah, I'm glad the dresses met with your satisfaction. Do you remember how you traded Mary last year for three horses and it took her several weeks to get paid off?"

"I do, Maggie, what do you have in mind?" Jonah was curious.

"Well I have Reece and Sam over at the livery looking at the used buggies and horses they have. I was wondering if you would get the buggy and horse and then I would pay you back in as many weeks as you see fit with the dresses, butter and eggs. How does that sound to you?" Maggie almost held her breath waiting for him to answer.

"I think it sounds great, Maggie. Let me leave Liv here in the store and I'll wander over to the livery and talk to Sam and Reece. We'll come up with a fair deal, I promise you. This will guarantee us getting dresses for many weeks to come!" Jonah laughed. He had always liked Maggie and knew she was good friends with Olivia, his wife and Mary Murphy. Their friendship got her through a very rough time in her life. She deserved some happiness and if getting her a horse and buggy will do it, then so be it! He'd make sure that it got done!

"Oh, Liv, I'm so excited! Just imagine, to have my own buggy and to be able to go out to see Mary whenever I want, it's just too good to be true. Put these dresses, butter and eggs on the purchase of the buggy and horse. Just tell me how many more weeks I've got to pay it off! I'll take a half dozen peppermint sticks and some rope and that should be it for now. I'll pay cash for those." Maggie told her friend.

"When are you planning on visiting Mary?" Liv asked while she counted out Maggie's change.

"We've plans to go berry picking tomorrow morning. Would you be able to come with us? You could take Josie and the three little girls, Josie, Andie and Kit will get to be good friends, plus we'll have extra hands picking all those berries. I really don't want Mary going out into the woods with the three little ones so close to her due date. We made a trip out last Friday, and it made Mary very tired. Cade doesn't like Mary to stray too far from the house. But with both of us, Cade won't have so many objections. What do you say?" Maggie asked.

"I'd love to, just let me check with Jonah. I know he'll love the fresh berries. Berry pie is his favorite. Plan on us going, unless I send Josie down with a message telling you otherwise. It will be so good to see Mary again after being cooped up all winter with the weather!" Liv told her as she walked out the door.

Maggie and the girls headed back to the house with the rope. Maggie told them when they got to the house, they could pass out the peppermint sticks to everyone, so they would be able to take a break. She was already planning on what to make for dinner.

CHAPTER 10

It was noon before Sam returned with the new buggy and horse. Maggie was thrilled! She ran out to greet them as soon as they drove into the back yard.

"Oh, Sam, I love them. What a beauty of a horse! Thank you, so much!" She hugged Sam when he climbed in to the buggy and she looked up at Sam just as he was looking down at her. It seemed the most natural thing in the world to come together with a kiss. It was the first time that Maggie had been kissed in almost nine years. She didn't count the ones that had been forced on her by men hoping to comfort a grieving widow. She was trembling, and she could feel Sam's heart beating. It had affected both of them. "I didn't mean to do that, Sam, I'm sorry..." Maggie whispered as she reluctantly pulled away from him.

"I'm not...I've been wanting to kiss you since the first day we came to town and you were shaking that derringer at that railroad man! I just didn't want you to point it at me." Sam told her grinning.

Maggie returned the grin and suddenly felt good about the kiss. She was joined quickly with Andie and Kit. "Oh, Maggie, isn't she beautiful! What should we call her?" Andie was stroking the face of the gentle mare. "I know! Let's call her Beauty, like in that book you read to me! Uncle Sam doesn't have a name for his horse, we'll call him Beast! Just like in the book, *Beauty and the Beast*!"

"Hey, wait a minute!" Sam grabbed Andie and lifted her up in his arms. "My horse is not an ugly Beast!"

"Maybe not, but until you come up with another name for him, Maggie and I will call him the Beast! Won't we, Maggie?" Andie told him laughing as he tickled her before he let her go.

"I like the sound of Beauty and Beast. Does Reece have a name for his horse? And we really do need a name for the cow. I'll let you girls think about names while I finish putting lunch on the table. I'll call Silas to come and put the buggy and the horse away. Thanks again, Sam, I can't tell you how much of a difference it will make for Andie and me to go pick berries and help Mary out when she has that baby!" Maggie disappeared into the house and Silas appeared shortly afterwards. He was grinning from ear to ear when he saw the horse and buggy.

"Miz Maggie be going in style when she go to the store from now on, won't she, Sheriff? That sure is a mighty fine rig. Let me take the little lady and put her in the corral with the rest of the horses. I'll park the buggy in the back of the barn. I'll get a stall ready for her in nothing flat. Things sure are changing around here right and left..." Silas continued to talk to himself and the new mare as he took them back to take care of them.

Sam looked around, he had to agree. He watched as Cam stacked wood carefully beside the house. He saw Chris plowing the garden plot that Maggie had staked out. He thought of Silas making the cellar a safe place for Maggie and of the buggy and the mare. Maggie would be able to get the supplies she needed all at once and visit with her friends as well. He loved seeing Andie playing with Kit or Josie, she was making friends and happy. She hadn't been happy since Andrew died. He gave a sigh and headed to the house to pick up sandwiches for Reece and himself. He needed to get back to work now that Maggie had her buggy. They had been arranging a good deal and then Jonah arrived and managed to get the price down even more when he told him he'd pay cash for the transaction. She'd be making dresses for the next two months to pay it off, but he didn't think she'd mind.

Maggie already had sandwiches, cookies and a jar of cool water from the well ready for him. He thanked her and headed back to work. He saw that she was still a little pink from the kiss and remembered all over again how good she felt in his arms. He had felt that kiss all the way to his toes. That Maggie was sure some woman, Sam thought.

By lunch, the wood had been stacked, the garden plowed, the stall readied for the mare and two walls were up for the cellar. Maggie was thrilled with the work done so far. The boys and girls and Silas ate everything she had made for lunch and all the cookies in her cookie jar. They had all worked up a hunger. While Maggie cleaned up the dishes from lunch, Cam and Chris started on the wash stand and Silas went back down to get the rest of the walls done in the cellar. He asked Andie and Kit to carry in planks and leave them at the door to the basement. He'd take it from there. The two girls were delighted to be able to help and set to it with laughter and giggles.

Cam and Chris had brought with them a grill for the top of the wash stand. Malachi Graham had forged it together at his blacksmith shop. It didn't take them long at all to dig a hole and to get the wash stand built. They also made a rectangular box next to it to put her rinse cauldrons on. Maggie loved it. They went in to make the bed next.

They used two by fours to make the frame and put planks on the four sides. They put smaller boards inside the box and laid planks to give the bed more support. They hammered in nails along both sides and wove rope back and forth to give the bed some leeway when anyone laid on the bed. Andie and Kit hammered the nails down securing the ropes. Maggie grabbed an extra sheet and sewed up three sides of the sheet. She and the boys went out into the tall grassy yard behind the barn and cut grass to fill the new mattress. Maggie sewed up the fourth side and put it on the new bed. She and Andie and Kit quickly made up the bed using sheets and the blanket and quilt they had used on the cot. It looked great and a lot sturdier than the cot ever was! Maggie was thrilled, and she gave each of the boys two dollars for all the work they had done for her. They didn't want to accept the money, but she insisted and asked them to bring her two more loads over the course of the summer and fall so she would have enough wood to last out the winter. They gladly agreed. They loaded up Kit and the plow and took off for home. They were looking forward to seeing them tomorrow when they came picking berries.

Maggie and Andie started planting their garden. They were able to get in the corn and the green beans before they stopped to make dinner. Maggie was making fried chicken and mashed potatoes for dinner in celebration of getting her new horse and buggy. She and Andie also had to make another batch of cookies to refill her cookie jar. Maggie hummed and sang while she worked in the kitchen.

Silas had finished all four walls of her basement/cellar. He still needed to put in the floor. He had had to shoot another snake and breathed a sigh of relief that the stairs were safely encased now with wood walls. He hoped that would be the end of the snakes. Maggie asked him to go to the lumber yard to get twelve one-inch by one-inch long sticks of wood to put in every corner of the cellar. With those in the corners, Maggie felt sure that they wouldn't have any more trouble with snakes. She gave Silas the money and he took off. If it would make Maggie happy, then Silas would just about do anything for her.

Reece and Sam loved the fried chicken and went back for seconds and thirds. Silas told them about killing the snake this morning and about Maggie wanting him to seal each of the corners with the one-inch by one-inch wood. Reece told him it would give the cellar a more finished look and give them all peace of mind to know that they wouldn't be encountering any uninvited guests every time them went down to get supplies. Sam wanted to check the outside of the house all along its base to see if they could see where they were getting into the house. If they could find the place, they could fill it up to stop the snakes getting into the basement in the first place.

Maggie told the three men that she and Andie would be going out to the Murphy's in the morning. She would leave lunch for Silas and have a lunch ready for Sam and Reece when they left in the morning. They would be back by early afternoon to work on finishing the garden. Silas told her that by the time she came back, he hoped to have her cellar done and ready to fill. She asked him to make her several shelves all along two sides. She wanted bins on one side and the remaining side they would take down and put all her extra supplies of flour, sugar, rice, beans and cornmeal. It would free up a lot of room in her kitchen. She would also stop by the General Store and start buying quart and pint jars. They would need them for the berries they were bringing with them to store the jam and berries for pies this fall and winter. Silas assured her, he'd have them ready so that they could fill them up. He also told her he'd help her and Andie finish planting their garden. Sam and Reece left to go out on their rounds. Sam wanted to find out the names of the two cowboys who had looked to be mocking them were. He felt like they could bear watching.

They weren't at the same saloon, but Sam questioned the bartender.

"Last night when we arrested the men who were shooting during the card game, there were two men sitting over at the last table. Do you know who they were?" Sam asked the bartender and owner of the saloon.

"You probably mean Jackson Slaughter and his buddy, Scott Lane. They're always looking for work but never seem to be short of money. They've been here off and on for about two years. They don't take much prodding before they pull their guns out. They're both lightning fast with those pistols. Why do you ask?" The bartender questioned.

"They stood out last night when we asked everyone to hand over their fire arms. I like to see my opponents and they looked like they weren't on board with the new rules." Sam told him.

"I'd say they both bear watching. I wouldn't turn my back on either one of them if I were you." The bartender warned them as they left the saloon.

Sam and Reece intended to do just that.

CHAPTER 11

Tuesday morning came bringing with it, bright sunshine but with storm clouds off in the distance. Maggie promised to be mindful of the clouds to Sam and Silas as they finished the morning chores and loaded the buggy with every container and bucket, she could find to fill with berries, mushrooms and wild onions. Maggie and Andie were both dressed in pants and a shirt. She left sandwiches for all three of the men and enough cookies to get them by until she got home and made them berry cobbler for dinner. Silas promised to put in the floor, the corner pieces and her shelves and bins. He'd be ready to help them plant the garden when they returned. Maggie hoped they'd finish the garden before it rained, so the gentle rain would help water the new seeds. She loved watching a garden grow and all her flowers, too.

She stopped at the General Store to pick up Olivia and Josie and all their buckets, too. Maggie asked Jonah to have some quart and pint jars ready when she returned. She'd be paying cash for them. She also told him she loved the horse and buggy he had helped bargain for and would make sure that she made all the dresses, butter and eggs in the next two months' worth it for all his hard work. Jonah just grinned and told her he was glad to see she was happy with her new acquisition!

Maggie and Olivia talked and chatted all the way out to the Murphy's. Josie and Andie giggled the entire way, you would have thought they had been friends for life the way they got along. Mary was ready with her cart and all her children. Cam and Chris would be going with them today because Cade was still plowing and planting the last of the crops. She hated to lose them to their father, because they were her muscle in getting a lot of her heavier jobs done.

It was a happy group that started off. They were going slower than usual because Mary was so very pregnant! She complained that she waddled when she walked! She also told the two women that Cade wasn't going to let her go berry picking by herself. He was worried that she would go into labor out in the woods all by herself and the children. He knew that Liv and Maggie would make sure that everything was alright.

They found berry bush after berry bush. With all of them picking it didn't take them as long as they thought it would to fill every container, they had brought with them. It was while they were walking back to the cabin that Mary's water broke. She looked up surprised at her two friends, at a loss for words. Maggie took charge.

"Chris, we're going to need you to handle the cart back to the cabin. Cam take off running and get your dad. When Chris gets back with the cart, you can both take off and get the doctor from town. When you get the doctor, tell the Sheriff and Silas and Jonah that Olivia and I will be late coming home today. Tell them your ma is having the baby and then hightail it back home. Andie, Josie and Kit take care of Cody and Cooper. Make sure they get home safely and then watch over them as we help Mary. Liv take one side of Mary and I'll take the other, we're going to help her get home as quickly as we can. Are you having any contractions yet, Mary?" Maggie asked her as she sent the boys hurrying off down the path towards home. She looked behind them and saw that the three girls had the little boys between them and were carefully taking care of them.

"My back has been sore for the last week and only a few contractions, nothing regular yet and nothing very strong. I'm confident we'll make it home before I have this baby. I'm a little worried, because it's a few weeks early. I don't want anything to happen to our baby!" Mary told them as they helped her walk.

"Now, Mary, you know that every baby is different just like every child is different. Liv and I will make sure that nothing happens that will hurt you or this baby. We'll stay and help the doctor and make sure that you are all delivered safe and sound. We'll feed your family while we're waiting and set up a schedule to come back each day and help you out until you're back up on your feet again." Maggie's words helped assure the expectant mother.

It seemed to take forever to get back to the cabin. By then Mary was having contractions on a regular basis. Maggie told Liv to run ahead and get the bed ready for Mary, she'd help Mary the rest of the way inside. Liv ran the rest of the way, calling out to the girls and little boys as she ran. "Josie, Kit, Andie fill the wood box in the cook stove and the fireplace! Kit where's your mother's extra old newspapers? Do you know if she has another oilcloth we can use for the bed?"

"Yes ma'am, I'll show you where everything is kept. Mama showed me where she put the newspapers and oilcloth the other day just in case, I'd be the one helping her get everything ready to have that baby! I'm really glad that you and Miss Maggie are here." Kit told her as she showed her where everything was. Liv had time to put down the oilcloth, newspapers and put a clean sheet over the entire surface. Then she put on a huge kettle of water. Mary and the new baby would need to be washed and cleaned.

Cade arrived as they came to the back porch. He didn't help Mary, he picked her up and carried her inside. He didn't care that two of her best friends were there, he kissed her on her forehead and then on her lips as he put her down. "Mary mine, are you doing alright? I would die if anything happened to you!" Cade told her in a frantic whisper.

"I'm doing just fine, love. Help me get out of these wet clothes and into a fresh nightgown. I'm not too steady on my feet right now." Mary told him with a smile that quickly turned into a grimace as another contraction gripped her body. "They're getting harder and stronger, Maggie. I don't think it will take as long with this one as it did with Benji."

Together, Cade and Maggie took off her wet clothes and then Maggie washed her from the top of her head to the bottom of her toes. They slipped the nightgown over her head and helped her lie down on the mattress. Maggie gave Mary and Cade a few minutes alone while she went out and helped Olivia get some lunch on the table for the three girls and the two little ones. They also made up sandwiches for Cam and Chris when they returned with the doctor. "Andie, when the five of you are done eating, would you go out into the cart and separate the berries and put all of Liv's and ours in the buggy. While we wait, Liv, we'll put up Mary's into quart jars for her. I don't want them to go to waste and she won't be in any shape to get them put up before they spoil."

"That's a good idea, Maggie, why don't I wash the jars and the berries and get them sealed while you concentrate on helping Maggie until the doctor gets here." Olivia volunteered.

"Sounds good, why don't you start a pot of coffee, I think Cade is going to need something to fortify him for the next few hours. The doctor will also be glad of a nice hot cup of coffee when he gets done delivering that baby!" Maggie squeezed Liv's shoulder as she hurried back into the bedroom.

Mary was already trying to push. "Mary! Don't push yet, the doctor isn't here." Maggie told her.

"I can't help it! This baby is in a big hurry to get here!" Mary told her between contractions.

Maggie went into high gear, she sterilized the scissors to cut the cord and readied the water to wash the baby once it was born. She put out a sleeper, diapers and booties to put onto the new infant. She told Cade to get some bricks and put them in the fireplace and get them warm. He also needed to get some towels to wrap the hot bricks in to put around the baby once it was born to keep it from getting chilled. After having gone through this five times before with his first wife, you would have thought that Cade was an old hand at helping to give birth to his children. But he wasn't! He felt like he was all thumbs as he readied the bricks and gave Mary encouragement.

Maggie had been nervous, but once she saw the head crowning her nervousness left and all she cared about was delivering a healthy baby and getting Mary through this safely and quickly. "Mary, I can see the head! It's got a mess of the blackest hair I've ever seen!" Even as Maggie talked to Cade and Mary, the baby slid right into Maggie's hands. She swept the mucus out of the baby's mouth and snipped the cord. The baby was a wiggling mess and about as slippery as an oiled pig. Maggie hadn't even had time to see if it was a girl or a boy, the baby hadn't taken a breath on its own and Mary slapped the little bottom to startle a cry out of the baby. It worked, and the little infant let loose with a bellow at being so rudely treated. Maggie, Cade and Mary all smiled at the beautiful sound.

"It's a boy! He looks to be a big boy for such a little lady such as yourself to be having! Let me get him all bundled up and then I'll take care of you, Mary. Cade come and hold him." Maggie issued commands as she tried to take care of the crying baby and Mary too.

Cade held the baby as if he were made of glass and could break at any instant! "He's beautiful, Mary! Another boy, can you believe it? Do you think Kit will be disappointed that she didn't get a sister?"

Maggie laughed as she helped with the afterbirth and cleaning up Mary, "I think she'll be so thrilled at having a baby in the house, she won't have time to be sorry about having a brother instead of a sister!" Maggie took the soiled sheet and oilcloth and wadded them up. She also took the bloody newspapers and left the room. She put the newspapers in the wash stand and started a fire to burn them and she put the sheets and oilcloth in water to soak. Then she carried in warm water to give the baby its first bath.

While she was washing the tiny fingers and toes and cleaning him up to present to his new parents, Maggie asked them what they were going to name the newest member of the Murphy clan.

"We decided on Charles Benjamin Murphy...Charlie for short. Charles was Mary's father's name and Ben was her first husband's and son's name. By calling him Charles Benjamin Murphy, he gets something from her past and her future. It's a way of always remembering Benji. He's gone but never forgotten. What do you think? Plus, his initials are still C.M. just like all the other children." Cade told her smiling as he held his wife gently in his arms.

"I think it's perfect, do you want to go tell the rest of your family or do you want me to?" Maggie asked as she settled the now clean and quiet baby into Mary's waiting arms. Tears were running down Mary's cheeks as she touched the little face and hands of her newest son. "Hello...Charlie...I'm your mama...and this handsome man is your father. I've waited a long time to hold a baby in my arms again. You are perfect, and your brothers and sister are going to love you and spoil you a lot...I love you...Charlie." Mary whispered softly to her new son. She looked up at Maggie, "Thank you, my friend, for helping me bring him into this world. I don't know what I would have done without you and Liv here to help."

"No thanks are needed. Just having a healthy baby and a smiling mother is all the thanks I need. I think I hear the boys and the doctor outside, I'll send him in and announce the baby's arrival." Maggie turned and left the room. She was so happy for Mary and at the same time was so jealous of all she had. Maggie wanted more than anything to have a houseful of children like Mary had. She didn't begrudge her friend her happiness, but she sure wished that some of it would rub off on her!

Just like Maggie told Cade, Kit didn't care what the baby was, she was just thrilled to be able hold a new baby in her arms. They all liked the name Charlie and were glad that their new ma was alright. Olivia and Maggie made them a big batch of beef stew and enough biscuits to feed an army. They had made up two cobblers and canned the rest of her berries. Doctor Mitcham told them that the baby and Mary looked to be in very good hands. He told the women and their girls to head back to town while it was still light out. He would stay until the next morning to make sure that there would be no surprises. Maggie told them she would head back the next day to take care of Mary, the new baby and the rest of the clan. Olivia would come the next day. Doc Mitcham told them they were lucky to have such good friends. Maggie and Olivia took off shortly afterwards. But not before they had kissed and got to hold the baby!

There was barely room for the four people in the buggy with all the berries. Maggie knew that even though she was tired, she would be making berry cobbler tonight and canning all these berries before she went to bed tonight! She hoped that Silas had finished the cellar and had even had time to start planting their garden. Maggie definitely wouldn't be working on it tonight or tomorrow what with helping Mary and her family. She gave a huge sigh of relief that everything had gone so well. God had been good to them and to her as he guided her through the birth process. She was really glad she didn't have to deliver a baby every day!

CHAPTER 12

After dropping off Olivia, Josie and all their berries, Maggie and Andie headed home. They were met by all three of her men. Reece and Sam carried in all the berries, Silas took Beauty and the buggy to the barn to be put away. Maggie immediately went into high gear, her 'family' was hungry, and she needed to make them something quick and filling to eat. It seemed like only minutes before she had fried potatoes, ham steaks and canned green beans on the table. Andie had been asked to help make biscuits and she had jumped at the chance. Maggie had taken over the remainder of the biscuit dough and dropped it on fresh berries mixed with sugar and flour. She popped it into the oven as they all sat down to eat. Andie held center stage as she told all about picking berries, helping Mary have a baby and helping take care of Cody and Cooper. She had loved feeling needed and playing with her friends all day. She couldn't wait to go back tomorrow and help them until Mary was back on her feet again.

"They named him Charlie! I like the name Charlie. I even got to hold the baby. He was all red and so tiny I couldn't believe it! Maggie helped him pop out of Mary's stomach...didn't you Maggie?" Andie told them.

Sam, Reece and Silas grinned at the idea of a baby popping out of any woman's stomach, "How'd it go, Maggie? Are you going to take up being a midwife next?"

"Not hardly! But the doctor wasn't there yet, and I really didn't have a choice! But I will agree with Andie, he was beautiful!" Maggie told them as she took the cobbler out of the oven. She served them up all good-sized portions and poured cream into the bowls over the bubbling mixture.

"I want to know how she can be gone all day picking berries and delivering babies and she still has time to fix us a great meal?" Sam asked the room at large.

"Maggie..." Andie began, "Why don't you have a baby? I'd sure like to have a baby around here just like Kit does. What do you think?" She looked up at Maggie with wide innocent eyes. She had no idea how much Maggie would like that to happen too, but she wasn't married anymore, and she didn't have any likely prospects wanting to put a ring on her finger.

"Well, Andie..." Maggie began turning all different shades of red as she blushed at the idea, "I would love to have a baby for us to love and spoil, but I don't have a husband. Both parents are needed to make a baby."

"How about Uncle Sam or Reece? They could marry you and then you could have the baby you want!" Andie looked at both her uncle and his friend. Their spoons of berry cobbler were both stopped half-way to their mouths. They were speechless at Andie's suggestion.

Silas grinned and added, "Sounds like a good-idea to me, too, Andie!" He was enjoying the two men's discomfort. "I could even put together a cradle for them."

"Andie, we'll talk about it sometime...but for now, I need to get back uptown for rounds. Great meal Maggie, thanks..." Sam said and rushed out the back door. Reece was hot on his heels.

"What did I say that they left even before their cobbler was done?" Andie asked them at large.

"I'm sure it wasn't anything you said..." Maggie told her. "Let's finish up here, we have a lot of berries to wash and put in jars and can before I can go to bed tonight. Do I dare ask if you two will help me get it done?"

"We sure will, won't we Andie! It means we'll be eating berry cobbler all winter long." Silas told her with his eyes twinkling. "I got everything planted in the garden except the potatoes and sweet potatoes. I'll do them tomorrow while you're out at the Murphy's. I should even have enough chicken wire to put up a little fence around the garden to discourage any critters from eating the fresh green shoots of the new plants. While you start the dishes, Andie and I will carry down the quart and pint jars, you won't be using tonight. Let's get started."

While Maggie washed the dishes and the quart and pint jars, she would be using, Silas and Andie washed the berries and removed any stems or leaves. All Maggie had to do was put them in jars and fill them with sugar water. Then she put them in the copper pot on the stove and let them sit in the steaming hot water for fifteen minutes to seal them. They sat on the counter when she was done so they could cool enough to go in her cellar. As soon as they were finished, all three of them headed off to bed. Maggie and Silas had another chuckle as to how fast Sam and Reece got out of the kitchen as soon as getting married was mentioned.

Maggie slept the sleep of the dead. She didn't hear Sam or Reece come in after rounds and thankfully, there were no unwanted visitors banging on the doors. As soon as Maggie woke up, she started up a batch of bread, big enough to have some for her hungry men and enough to feed Mary's household, too. Then she collected the dirty clothes and started up the wash stand. Silas brought in the milk and the eggs and told her he'd be back in after he cleaned out the stalls and let the animals out for the day.

Maggie took a few minutes to make up a very large batch of biscuits and gravy and also fried up some bacon. She made bacon sandwiches for her three men to eat while she was gone for the day and started up a large batch of chili to eat for dinner. Sam and Reece came in and ate several helpings of the biscuits and gravy.

"I made you bacon-biscuit sandwiches for lunch and there's still the berry cobbler that you didn't finish last night to go with it." Maggie teased the two men.

"Sorry to leave you with some explaining to do...I haven't been around little girls before. I didn't know how to tell her about babies or marriage or love or any of that stuff! I thought the best way was to get out as quickly as we could, I sure did hate missing that cobbler! How did it go with explaining things to Andie?" Sam asked cautiously.

"Fine," Maggie told him with a grin. "Silas and I just changed the subject! You still get to tell her everything she might want to know about the birds and the bees..." Maggie burst out laughing. "I think she's a little young to ask the big questions yet, she is only six after all. But you might want to tell her that people have to fall in love before they get married and have babies. That should satisfy her for a few weeks...at least!"

Sam nodded and smiled back. It's not that he had anything against marriage, he just never figured on getting married himself. As a U.S. Marshall, he was constantly on the go. That was no way to have a good marriage. Now that he was a Sheriff and not a U.S. Marshall, he had a more stable job, but there was still a lot of risk being a sheriff. He could get shot and leave a wife with a bunch of kids. He didn't like that picture either. He wasn't sure how he was going to raise Andie by himself, but he'd take each day one at a time. Hopefully, Maggie would continue to help him sort things out by looking after Andie. He could see a big difference just in the short time they had lived in her house. She talked more and smiled all the time. He really felt like she was content with things the way they were. He sure was. It didn't mean that he didn't like kissing Maggie and getting to know her a lot better. But they had time, lots and lots of time.

Maggie washed up their dishes and reminded them that she would be going out to Mary's today to help with the baby. She and Andie would get back late but hopefully before dinner. Sam advised her to get back before it got dark. As soon as Cade got in from the fields, she and Andie needed to hightail it back to town. He told her that they would be looking out for them. Maggie liked having someone worry about them, it had been a long time since anyone cared when she got back to town.

CHAPTER 13

As Andie and Maggie headed out of town, she stopped at the General Store to order more quart and pint jars. She would try to pick them up on the way home. Andie was a chatterbox all the way out to the ranch. She really liked playing with Kit and even liked taking care of Cody and Cooper, her little brothers. Maggie knew that she would need to give Mary and Charlie baths this morning. She knew that there had to be a ton of wash to do taking care of six children and all those diapers! She needed to make up a batch of bread and a big pot of chili for their dinner. Sandwiches would do just fine for lunch. She wondered if she would have time to pick more berries and weed Mary's vegetable garden. Her garden had been in for several weeks and Maggie knew that it needed to be weeded several times a week. It looked to be a very busy day for her and the children.

Cade was still at the cabin when Maggie got there. She looked at the lumpy mush he had made for their breakfast and laughed. Maggie told Chris to take it out and see if the pigs would eat it! She started up another kettle to make them breakfast. She had mush ready in minutes and bacon frying. Biscuits were slid into the oven even as Chris, Cam and Cade declared that her mush was much better than Cade's had been! She quickly made them sandwiches to take with them.

"Cade, I'm going to give Mary and Charlie a bath this morning and wash clothes. I'll fix a big kettle of chili for dinner. Do you see any problems with my taking the two little boys and the two girls out to do a little more berry picking? I'll go while Mary and Charlie are sleeping, and we won't go very far. I just know that berries don't last for very long and Mary always said to pick when the picking was good!" Maggie told Cade as he packed up to finish the fields.

"I see no problem with any of that. Maggie. Just don't try to do too much. Whatever doesn't get done today, we can finish tomorrow. I would like if you took a rifle with you. Bears like berries, too! If you need us, just fire the rifle a few times. The boys and I will take off and be with you in a shot. Thanks for everything, Maggie, we really do appreciate everything you did last night and again today. You're a good friend." Cade told her with a hug.

"Oh, get on with you! Friends don't have to tell each other thank you! You wouldn't let me tell you thank you last fall when Stephen died. Where would I have been without you and Mary, Olivia and Jonah, Wes and Lily and my sister, Brenda? You saved me and got me through a very rough winter! I love you guys and Andie loves being a part of a big family. She even asked me if I might have a baby and asked Sam and Reece to marry me! You have never seen two grown men move so fast! They were up and out the door before they even finished their dessert! Silas and I laughed for quite a while over that! Now get going, those fields aren't going to plant themselves!" Maggie waved as the three took off.

First Maggie and Andie went into see Mary and Charlie. She had just fed him, and he had fallen back asleep. Maggie took the opportunity to feed Mary the newer mush she had made. Then she helped her take a bath and changed the sheets on the bed. She started up the wash stand, and then she started washing diapers, sheets and dirty clothes for the entire family. Andie played in the yard with their dog while she waited for Kit and the boys to wake up.

When the three children woke up, Maggie fed them and made all the beds in the loft. She gave Charlie a bath and changed his bedding in his cradle. She made sure to ask Cody and Cooper to hand her things she used on the baby, so they would feel important. Kit held the baby while Andie and Maggie washed up the breakfast dishes. They put him in his clean cradle and then Kit helped Maggie put together a large kettle of chili. Maggie scrubbed the kitchen floor with the last of the wash water and asked the children to load up all the buckets they were going berry picking. Maggie told Mary to take a nap, they wouldn't be gone long.

The children loved taking the cart out and picking berries. The woods behind the Murphy's cabin held an abundance of berries, and Maggie even found some rhubarb and wild onions and mushrooms. They filled every container they had brought and had even eaten a pretty good number of them as well. Maggie was guiding the cart and Kit held Cooper's hand while Andie held Cody's hand. They were singing as they marched along. They were almost home when Maggie heard the horrible sound of growling coming from the wooded area to the left of them. She reached for the rifle and even patted her pocket to make sure the derringer was safe just in case! She moved the children behind the cart and herself. She would stand between whatever was crashing into every tree and bush it came across. Maggie couldn't fathom what could be making such a noise.

It was a wolf. A lone wolf with foam dripping from its mouth. It looked to be sick, it could hardly stand and kept crashing into everything that stood in its path. Maggie was scared. She knew what the foam meant. The wolf had hydrophobia. It had to be killed before it got too close to them. Maggie raised her rifle to her shoulder and said a silent prayer. 'Please God, don't let me miss! Help me keep these children safe!" With that she pulled the trigger!

Maggie fired several times before she was convinced that the wolf was dead. Now came the problem of getting rid of the body! If they burned the carcass, they could start a fire that would burn the entire woods and cabin and barn down. But they did have to keep other wild animals from eating the carcass. It could further spread the disease. They could be looking at an epidemic. She had the children start digging in the soft dirt of the forest floor. They would bury the wolf and cover it with rocks to help other animals from getting sick. The children seemed to sense the emergency and they all dug frantically.

It was Maggie who heard the thunder of several horses running toward them. "Maggie! Maggie can you hear me? Is everyone all right?" Cade called as they rode.

"Over here, Cade!" Maggie stood up and waved her apron to attract their attention.

One look told Cade all he needed to know. The animal had rabies. It was deadly and had to be destroyed. "Did...any of you touch it?" Cade asked and looked to Maggie for an answer.

Everybody started talking at once! They were excited, they were scared, and they were so glad that their pa had showed up to make sure that everything was all right! "No one had touched it. We were in the midst of digging a hole to push the wolf's body in with some sticks. We were going to cover it with dirt and then rocks to make sure no other animal will get what it's got." Maggie took a long trembly sigh. "Am I ever glad that you told me to take the rifle with me today, Cade! I'm not sure that my little derringer would have stopped the wolf..." Maggie let her sentence sort of drift away, both she and Cade were imagining all sorts of gruesome scenes in their minds of what could have happened.

Cade was the first to take charge. "Chris take the cart up to the house. Let your mother know that everything is all right, she'll be worried hearing the shots. Then get several shovels out of the barn and bring them back to us. When you get back with them, I'm going to send you and Cam, to town to alert the Sheriff. If there's one sick animal with hydrophobia, there's bound to be more. He's got to alert every farmer and rancher around us and also the town. If we're not careful, a lot of people could get hurt over this. It might even cost some of them their lives. Cam, you and the other kids start bringing all the rocks you can see in the immediate area. I want you all to stay within seeing distance. Maggie and I will dig a hole for the wolf and cover it with dirt. We're going to have to bury him deep, so the other animals won't dig him up. Then we have to put all those rocks over him. Let's get busy..." He paused as they all went in different directions. "It seems like I have to thank you again Maggie for saving my children. I don't...know...what I ...would do, if anything happened to them." There were tears in Cade's eyes as he looked at Maggie. Maggie just nodded her head, she couldn't have spoken a word, she had a huge lump in her throat.

When Chris came back with the shovels, Cade had even more instructions for he and Cam. "Get a rifle from the house and take it with you. Make sure it's loaded. When you let the Sheriff know what happened, let them know that Maggie and Andie will be late getting back tonight. Taking care of this wolf, is going to slow all our jobs down a lot. Be careful boys, shoot anything that is not acting like a wild animal does. Most will run away from us, but if acts like it's going to attack, shoot to kill." The boys nodded and took off, they loved riding their horses and to carry an important message to the Sheriff made them feel really grown up. They'd get the job done as fast as they possibly could.

The shovels helped dig a hole for the wolf a lot faster. The pile of dirt and the pile of rocks kept getting bigger and deeper. Finally, Maggie and Cade picked the wolf up with the shovels, being careful not to touch the animal with their hands. They covered the wolf with the dirt and then all the children and Maggie and Cade put the rocks over the hole. They were filthy, but they were all right. They headed back to the cabin together.

Maggie had them start washing off the dirt in the barn. She didn't want the dirt to come anywhere close to Mary and the baby. Cade agreed, but as soon as he was clean, he took off to explain to Mary what had happened and that they were all perfectly all right. Maggie was cleaning up the children.

Maggie had Kit and Andie unload the berries. They took half into the Murphy cabin and the other half they put in Maggie's buggy. They all sat down to eat sandwiches. Mary understood that they were just fine, but it didn't stop her from calling every single child into her bedroom to check them over and give each of them a hug. She just kept saying over and over, "Thank you, God! Thank you, God!" Her tears poured down her face as she looked over their heads at her friend. "God bless you Maggie for being here! That wolf wasn't that far from our home! It could have attacked any of our animals or the children while they were outside playing! My hands won't stop shaking! I don't dare hold Charlie right now, I'd probably drop him!" Mary told them.

They finally settled down. Cade went out to work in his fields but not before he loaded the rifle that Maggie had used and put it where she could get to it again if she needed to. He loaded his six-guns and put on his belt. They would not be unprepared the next time! Maggie cleaned up the kitchen and then took the children and the rifle to the garden to start weeding. She needed to stay busy so that she couldn't think about what had happened.

The boys, Cam and Chris, came back from town and they were not alone. Sheriff Sam Kincaid rode with them. Their horses were lathered because they had ridden fast and furious to get back to the cabin in a hurry. Sam almost jumped out of his saddle and ran to Maggie. He grabbed her and kissed her, "My God! Are you sure that you're all alright?" Maggie could feel him tremble beneath her hands. It felt so good to have his strong arms around her to lean on. It had been quite some time since she had depended on anyone but herself.

"I'm so glad you're here, Sam...we buried the...wolf, so other wild animals couldn't get to it. Do you think...there are more of them out there?" Maggie asked him with her head on his shoulder.

"That's what I'm going to find out. I'm going to go to each farm and ranch in the area and warn them about the rabies. I'll find out if any of them have seen anything out of the ordinary. Reece is spreading the word in town. Silas said to tell you that he's finished the garden and already has a small fence around it. He'll be on the watch for anything unusual around the house and for you not to worry about a thing. Do not head back into town! I will return here when I finish my rounds and escort both you and Andie back into town tonight. Do you understand?" Sam finally took his arms away, but still held onto her with his hands.

Maggie nodded and said, "Thank you, Sam. Andie and I will wait right here for you to return. I promise." She looked up at him with her beautiful eyes clouded with unshed tears. It was Sam's undoing, he had to kiss her again before he climbed back into the saddle to start spreading the word about the rabies. Maggie was sure some woman to kill a rabid wolf and help her friends out so well. He wasn't sure what he was going to do about Maggie, but he knew he sure liked having her around!

CHAPTER 14

By the time the garden was weeded, the clothes on the line were dry and ready to be put away. Maggie kept the children close enough to see what they were doing. She didn't want anything to creep up on them when they weren't looking. She kept checking on Mary and little Charlie. They seemed to be doing well. Maggie stirred the chili several times and then started on making a cobbler for dinner and canning the rest of the berries. She even had enough berries to start up a batch of jam.

She had Kit and Andie wash out clean quart and pint jars and she had Cody and Cooper keep her wood boxes filled. She went with the children to gather the eggs and milk the cow. Together they filled the animals' water containers and gave them all grain and fresh straw from the loft. By the time Cade and the boys came in from the fields, the only thing they would have to do is brush down their horses and put them in their stalls. Maggie knew that it had been a long day for all of them. She didn't know if Sam would want to eat before they headed back to town or to wait until they got home to eat. She only set the table for the Murphy's.

She carried in a tray for Mary and took the chance to hold and rock Charlie. She let Andie hold him for a little while and then helped Cody and then Cooper hold their new little brother. She was sitting in the rocker singing softly to Charlie with the rest of the children playing on the floor at her feet when Sam returned. He couldn't take his eyes off the sight of Maggie holding the baby in the rocker. It sure looked and felt right to watch her. You could tell she liked children. Having a half dozen didn't seem to faze her and being able to hold the baby made her even more content. It gave Sam a lot to think about.

Maggie didn't want to leave until Cade returned from the fields. Sam wanted to leave before it got dark, it would be safer that way. Maggie won. She got up and gave Charlie to Sam and told him she was going to put away the cooled down berry containers to the cellar. Andie, Kit, Cody and Cooper helped her. They were just finishing up when Cade and the boys arrived back to the cabin. They put their horses away and noticed all that Maggie had done in their absence. It was nice not having to milk, gather eggs, or feed and water the animals. Chris and Cam thought that every muscle in their body ached after helping Cade all afternoon and morning. That bed would sure feel good. Maggie dished out the chili and put the crackers in the middle of table. She had the cobbler on the counter and told Kit it was ready to serve as soon as they finished their dinner. She took Charlie from Sam and put him in his cradle and covered him up with a small quilt. She kissed Mary good-bye and told them that Olivia would be coming out in the morning. She'd be back day after tomorrow. Within minutes, they were in the buggy with Beast tied up and trailing behind.

Andie was tired. They had gotten up early to finish all their chores before they left to go to the Murphy's. She laid her head in Maggie's lap and was asleep before they had gone more than a mile down the road. Maggie pushed her damp hair away from her face and lovingly covered her with her own shawl to keep her warm in the night air. Sam kept giving her covert glances. She was some woman all right, pretty and soft like women were supposed to be, smart and courageous when she had to be and at all times, she was loving to everyone she encountered. Sam was giving serious thought to making his relationship with Maggie a little more permanent. But he didn't know how she would feel about it. He was afraid to find out.

Maggie was deep in thought, too. It was so nice having Sam giving her support. It was really nice to be able to lean on somebody else for a change. He wasn't like her first husband at all, he was somebody you could depend on. He was so good to Andie and it was fun to see him holding little Charlie! He acted like he was about to drop him, and he would break if he held him too tight. At the same time, he had smiled down on the tiny hands and face and seemed to enjoy it. Maggie was afraid that she was beginning to like his kisses too much and she was beginning to depend on him too much. It could only lead to heartbreak for her and she had had enough of that to last her a lifetime. She knew in her heart that he would leave, it might not be today or even next week, but she knew that he was not a settling kind of man that wanted a wife and kids to tie him down. He was putting on a brave front for Andie, but she wondered how long he could keep it up. And then there were those kisses he kept giving her! They thrilled her all the way to her toes, she didn't want them to stop she liked them too much. They made her remember that she was still a woman, a rather old woman of thirty long years! She was no spring chicken to fall into the arms of the first man to grab her interest in nine years! He hadn't tried anything more than to kiss her. He hadn't tried to get in her bed like most of the men in town did because she was a 'lonely' widow starved for male attention. Maybe he wasn't interested in her in that way. She was probably too old for him to want her in that way. He was good-looking enough to get any woman he wanted in the town, why would he be interested in someone like her? Maggie gave a long sigh. Having Sam interested in her was not going to happen, she needed to start realizing that she was going to spend the rest of her life on the outskirts of her friends' lives. It would just have to be enough.

Sam heard her sigh, "It's been a long day hasn't Maggie?"

"Yes, it has, Sam. Did you get all the farms and ranches notified about the rabies in the area?"

"I did. Only two of the entire area had seen anything out of the ordinary. They had killed the animals and buried them just like you and Cade did. They were afraid of starting a range fire if they tried to burn them. They're going to let me know if they see anything more. I'd be surprised if the wolf and the two other animals were the only three in the area infected. You make sure that even in town that you and Silas stay alert of anything that isn't acting normal. I'd rather kill an innocent dog than have a single man, woman, or child get infected. You can bet that Reece and I will stay on our guard watching for anything that remotely resembles rabies." Sam paused and then stole another glance at Maggie. "It scared the hell out of me when I heard that a rabid wolf came at you and the children in the woods. Chris told us you didn't hesitate to shoot the animal. That took some amazing courage to keep those children safe."

"I wasn't courageous at all!" Maggie cried out in anguish. "I was so scared I was afraid that I would miss! I kept blaming myself for even putting them in harm's way in the first place! It was my idea to go berry picking and go off in the woods. It was Cade who told me to take a rifle with me, because bears like berries too! What if it had been a bear? I'm not so sure that the rifle would have stopped something that large unless you know where to hit it with a bullet. I don't! What if something had gone wrong and my shots had missed? So many things to worry about, and I didn't think about them at all. It was unforgiveable to take them out in the woods by myself! I should be the one shot or locked up! I am so sorry that I put Andie's life in danger, Sam. I will understand if you feel you have to find someone else to take care of Andie. But I have to tell you that I will sure miss having her around...I've fallen in love with her completely!"

"Maggie, you're not speaking anything worth saying! Anyone could have gone berry picking and they might not have had the good sense to grab up the rifle and kill the rabid wolf! We could have had an entirely different set of circumstances to deal with. If that wolf had bitten anyone, it's a death sentence! People go crazy, they go insane and then they die. If you hadn't been there today, that wolf could have gone down to the homestead and still gotten to one of the children before it was killed. I for one will go down on my knees to thank God that you were the one with those children today. You saved them with your quick thinking and actions. I wouldn't dare try to take Andie out of your care! Andie would probably shoot me in my sleep. She loves you too, Maggie. I think she thinks of you as the mother she has never known." Sam paused, "And I think we're both blessed to have found you to help us out. You have made the boarding house a home not a rented room. We all feel welcome not like we're just taking up space in your big old house. Andrew, my brother and Andie slept in the same room in Cheyenne for over five years and they never felt like it was home. Andie will tell you that women were only nice to her to get in good with her father. She can see through a phony a mile away. You two hit it off from the very first. You cared about her and about us. Don't ever think about throwing us out of your house, we plan on staying there forever if you'll let us."

"Oh, Sam, I could never send you or Andie away! It would be like cutting off my own arm and my heart. I love you all staying at my house, it's like I finally have a family like everyone else...It's what I've always wanted. You've given that to me. Thank you for letting me take care of you all! You give my very boring existence a reason for living." Maggie smiled at Sam as he took her hand and held it all the way back into town.

The rabies scare held the town in terror for over three weeks. Maggie and Olivia went out to the Murphy's for the first week until

Mary was up and doing for herself. But every time they went and then came back, they had either Reece or Sam riding with them. Jonah couldn't leave his store and it made him feel so much better that someone was with his wife when she went out into the hillside to help the Murphy's. Riding back and forth with Sam, gave Maggie and Sam lots of time to talk about a lot of subjects.

Maggie found out how Sam became a U.S. Marshall (his uncle had been a Texas Ranger and he had always admired him and wanted to be like him) and how many brothers and sisters he had. (One brother and his only sister died of pneumonia when she was only about nine years old.)

She found out that his parents were dead. (They had died when Sam was only fifteen years old and had never met Andrew's wife or his daughter.) He had never been in love or wanted to get married. (He did tell her that his thoughts on the subject were changing. He had never thought that he was a settling man, but he liked coming home to the same bed every night and finding great meals waiting for him. He especially liked coming home to such a pretty woman every night.) And she found out that Sam enjoyed kissing her as much as she enjoyed kissing him.

Sam found out that it was just Maggie and her older sister, Brenda. He found out about how Maggie and Brenda got Mary and Cade together after both their spouses died. Maggie told him all about Stephen and the ten years they had been married. Her parents had both died many years before, they would have been heart-broken to know the young man they had picked out for Maggie was such a low-life. Maggie never told them. Brenda knew, because she had visited her several times in the ten years that she was married. Sam also found out how much it hurt Maggie not to have any children to love and spoil.

Sam kissed Maggie every chance he got. He tried not to do it in front of Andie, so that she wouldn't get any ideas of matchmaking between them. But he felt like he was drawn to her. Just kissing was getting to be a bit of a frustration for him. He would have liked to do more than just kiss her, but he also knew that she wasn't that kind of woman. He was glad she wasn't that kind of woman and it sure made it difficult for him too. He was in between a rock and a hard place. But he would be all right. He just knew that as long as Maggie was there, everything would be alright.

The town of Pine City got lucky. Several wild animals were killed on the suspicion that they had rabies, but no one was bitten, and they didn't lose any lives over the epidemic. Spring rains helped the gardens flourish and the crops fill out to make them think it was going to be a bumper crop for all of them. It was the middle of June when all hell broke loose!

CHAPTER 15

The middle of June was warm and dry. Maggie had been diligent about weeding her garden and Silas had been a god-send about watering it. It was thriving! Andie was so thrilled to see something grow where she had only planted tiny seeds. She couldn't wait to start eating from the garden and canning. She fully intended in helping Maggie pick every green bean and corn cob she could find. Reece and Sam were relaxing their guard a bit from the rabies scare.

It was mid-morning when Malachi Graham and Mitch Drew showed up at the Sheriff's office. They wanted to report some cattle rustlers. There were about nine ranchers that wanted to report the loss of five or six cattle a piece. That made up a herd of at least fifty cattle. It was too much of a loss for any of the ranchers to absorb without feeling the pinch. Sam immediately grabbed his hat and told them he was going to get his horse and ride out and take a look, but first he wanted to let his Deputy know where he was going and what was going on. He was due to come into the office in a few hours.

He told Malachi and Mitch to follow him home and they would head out together. It took only minutes for Sam to yell at Silas to catch Beast and help him saddle him up. Maggie handed him a bag to put in his saddle bags of lunch for him to eat. She and Andie waved as the three men headed out of town. They were only gone minutes when they heard what sounded like hundreds of bawling cattle running towards town. It looked like a cattle stampede heading right for the middle of Pine City! Mitch, Malachi, and Sam switched directions and were going to try to head them off.

Silas heard the bawling of all the cows as well, he told Maggie to head into the house with Andie and take cover. He was going to batten down the animals just in case the cattle came towards their homestead. Silas had seen what was left after thundering hooves had just about wiped out an entire town in Colorado. He didn't want anything bad to happen to any of Miz Maggie's property if he could help it.

When Sam and the two ranchers met up with the stampeding cattle, they started firing their six-guns in the air in the hope to divert them from heading straight into town. Sam didn't want anyone to get hurt or any property destroyed. He noticed that there was a masked man in the back of the herd firing his gun keeping the herd in a frantic rush. Sam couldn't recognize who it was, but they were creating a lot of problems for the town.

They were managing to corral most of the cattle into stopping before they did too much damage. Several men came out to help them. That's when Sam heard the gun shots coming from the middle of town. The entire fiasco was just a diversion, so someone could rob the banks in town. Sam left the cattle to the ranchers and headed back to town to see if he was going to be in time to catch them.

There were two of them and they had been busy. They had robbed the Pine City First National Bank and the Pine City Bank! They were just trying to leave the Pine City Bank when Sam started firing at them. They still had their bandanas up as masks and Sam had no idea who they were. He was able to shoot one of the robbers and he fell off his horse with two of the money bags, he also hit the other robber, but he got away. But not before he returned fire at the Sheriff. Sam was hit in the shoulder. By then, Reece had joined the chaos. He quickly fired after the fleeing fugitive. Then he turned his attention to his partner, the Sheriff.

Sam was unconscious. Reece tore off his shirt and used it to try and staunch the flow of blood. He yelled at someone to go get the Doc! Doctor Mitcham came quickly and asked several by-standers to help carry Sam's body over to his office, so he could operate and get the bullet out. Reece ran over and turned the robber over and found him dead. He pulled the bandana down to see if he recognized the robber. He was a little shocked to discover it was Scott Lane. He figured the other robber had to be Jackson Slaughter. He had no idea who was instrumental in getting the cattle to stampede.

Reece sent someone to get the undertaker for the dead body, asked Bart Murray of the Pine City Bank to take possession of the bags of money and count how much was taken and how much was recovered. Then he sent Oliver Clark, the older son of Jonah and Olivia, to run over and tell Maggie that Sam had been shot in an attempted bank robbery. Doc Mitcham was going to operate as soon as possible.

Then he ran to the Doctor's office to see how Sam was faring and find out his chances of survival from the doctor. He wanted to give Maggie and Andie some good news when they arrived. He knew they would both be shaken up by seeing all the blood on Sam's shirt and hearing about a bank robbery. He was right.

Maggie and Andie had run all the way. They were pale and silent tears ran down both their faces. Doc Mitcham saw them arrive and started shouting orders.

"Maggie does the sight of blood make you sick to your stomach or dizzy?" Doc asked her as he started cutting off the shirt of Sam.

"No...why do you ask?

"Because I need some help in getting Sam taken care of and you're elected. Andie is too young, and I assume that Reece will need to go after the one that got away! Now, roll up those sleeves and wash those hands and arms with the glycerin soap by the sink.

Then put on a big pot of boiling water. These instruments need to be put in the boiling water and taken out, so I can use them. Clean instruments don't leave behind any germs that can cause infection. While you're doing that, Andie start tearing strips of that cloth over there in about five-inch width strips. We'll use them to help wrap up your Uncle. Get moving people!" Doc barked.

Andie and Maggie jumped to do his bidding. They wanted to feel they were helping in some way however small it might be. Maggie wasn't sure how she would hold up when she saw the Doctor cut into Sam, but if it would help keep him alive, she'd do whatever it took to get the job done.

The doctor and Maggie worked for over two hours getting the bullet and every piece of material or debris they could find in the wound. Then they had to disinfect the wound and finally sew up the hole in his chest. Sam never woke up while they were working on him. Doc said it was a good thing he was out, he didn't have the time to fight with him over staying still while he was operating!

By the time they were finished, Maggie's back hurt from bending over holding the light for the doctor. She could imagine how he felt. Sam was bandaged from his shoulder to almost his waist with white strips of cloth. His arm was immobile, so it couldn't be moved and tear out the stitches. Doc washed the blood off his own hands and arms.

"You did real well, Maggie! You would make a first-class nurse to help me out when I need it. Are you ready to change professions from boarding house to nursing?" He asked teasingly.

"Not a chance, Doctor! Will Sam be alright?" Maggie asked as she washed off her hands. She noticed that her apron and dress were pretty much covered with blood, Sam's blood.

"He should be if we can get him to stay in bed and recuperate! That will be the hard part, if I thought it would help, I'd tell you to tie him to the bed posts. You're going to play hell on wheels to keep that man down. He's going to want to go out and track down the man who shot him and stole from his town. It's not going to be good enough that he has a very good Deputy who can take care of things until he's feeling much better. You are going to have your hands full with that one!" Doc warned her.

Maggie gave him a smile, Sam would live. "Doc getting shot will be easy compared to trying to get past me and get out of bed. I may look soft and only be a woman, but you just wait and see, I'll keep Sam in bed even if I have to steal all his clothes to keep him there!"

Doctor Mitcham nodded his head, Maggie McDonald might have a heart of gold, but she had a spine of steel. His money was going to be on Maggie in keeping Sam in bed until he healed! The good doctor arranged for several neighboring men to carry Sam to his house and into bed. Maggie made them put him in her own bed on the first floor. It would be a lot easier checking on Sam and keeping an eye on him when he was so near the kitchen. She would be making up some broth and getting some liquids into him as soon as Silas got her some reeds she could hollow out and use as straws to get fluids down him. She'd even add some sage and honey to keep any fever down and reduce the risk of him going into shock. Doctor Mitcham would be coming over several times a day to check on his patient and give Maggie any medicine he needed to take. Maggie said several prayers of thank you to God for letting them help Sam and letting him live. Maggie didn't know what she would do without him and she didn't ever want to try.

She gathered up Andie and held her on her lap in one of the rockers in her parlor. Maggie told Andie over and over again, that Sam was going to be all right. She praised her for helping make bandages for the doctor. "Together Andie, we're going to help your uncle get better. You and I are going to be his legs for a few days. I'll sleep on the couch in the parlor, so that I can hear him in the night should he need me. While I'm in the kitchen or washing dishes, you can keep an eye on him and let me know what he needs. I do know that he'll probably be grumpy having to stay in bed. But we'll overlook that won't we?" Maggie told her in a soothing voice.

"Maggie, I was so scared! I thought that Uncle Sam would die just like my dad and mom did and I would be all alone! I'm so glad that I've got you to help take care of me and my Uncle Sam! I love you Maggie!" A very tearful Andie told Maggie as she hugged her tight.

"Oh, Andie, I love you, too! I don't ever want to think about you going anywhere else. This is your home...I love having you and your Uncle and Reece and Silas here with us. We're a family, a rather strange family but a family all the same." Maggie hugged Andie and then they both got up to start getting things ready to help Sam.

Maggie used her knitting needles to help hollow out the reeds to help Sam drink. She started up a kettle of broth from some meat she had in the smoke house. While she was at it, she started up dinner for the rest of them. She knew that Reece would be hungry after chasing down the robbers all afternoon and doing his job and Sam's. Silas went downtown and managed to find Beast and bring him home. He brushed him down and let him loose in the corral to eat with the cow and Beauty, Maggie's horse. Reece's horse was gone, so it looked like he was hunting the escaped robbers.

When Silas reported about Reece, Maggie said a silent prayer for his safe return. Maggie had Andie make up a batch of her special biscuits to go with the meal she was preparing to keep her busy. She also used the leftover biscuit dough to put on the top of the peach cobbler she was making up from a can of peaches. At least they would have a filling meal, Maggie thought. She or Andie were constantly going to see if Sam had awakened yet. Maggie checked to see if he were running a fever or getting chilled, all the things the Doctor had told her to be wary about. So far, so good, Sam wasn't awake, but he didn't look to be coming down with an infection or fever. Maggie would take one day at a time and pray for the best.

CHAPTER 16

Reece did not find Jackson Slaughter or his accomplice. It started to rain and washed out all the tracks until Reece couldn't tell which ones the robbers were, and which ones were only people coming in or out of Pine City. He got both banks to tell how much money was lost and how much of the money recovered was accounted for. Michael Hunt from the First National Bank told them that they lost over seven thousand dollars. Bart Murray of the Pine City Bank told him they lost just over five thousand dollars, but it was all accounted for in the two bags that they recovered from the dead robber. Hunt wanted them to split the recovered money, but since it was in Pine City Bank bags, Reece told him it remains with the Pine City Bank. Hunt was not a happy man.

Reece sent wires to the neighboring towns giving the description of Jackson Slaughter and letting him know that he was injured and might be seeking the help of their town's doctor. He wanted to be kept appraised of any and all sightings of the suspect.

Malachi and Mitch sorted through the cattle in the stampede and they were indeed the cattle that had been stolen from the nine ranches. With a little help from some of the cowboys in town, they herded them back home and delivered them to the ranchers who had reported them missing. They were able to sort them easily enough just by looking at the brands they all wore. The ranchers were very appreciative to get their livestock back. In taking Cade's cattle back to him they told him about the rustlers, the stampede and the Sheriff getting shot. He also passed on the word about the missing robbers and to be on the lookout of anyone suspicious in the vicinity.

Mary talked Cade into going into town to see how the Sheriff was doing and to also check on Maggie and Andie. She was worried how she was coping with everything that was going on in her own house and town. Cade had Chris and Cam arm themselves with a rifle and to guard the house and other buildings on their property. He didn't want anything happening to his family while he was in town checking on Sam.

By the time that Cade arrived in town, Sam was awake. He felt like hell and didn't look much better. He was pale from blood loss and somebody took all his clothes and wouldn't give him anything to put on but short johns. He was not happy. He felt like he should be up and doing his job.

"Sam, you are not going anywhere until the doctor says you can! I'm washing your clothes and will sew them up where the doctor had to cut them off you to operate. When they are clean, I will put them in your room. Until them, you are going to stay in that bed even if I have to tie you down! I want no arguments from you about this." Maggie paused and told him in a much softer voice, "We almost lost you Sam and neither Andie nor I could imagine being here in this house without you. Please let us take care of you. I know you want to hunt the robbers down, but they'll still be out there when you're well. Are you going to be reasonable about this?"

"I guess I'll have to be! Unless I want to walk through your house naked to get to my room and my clothes!" Sam even managed a smile. "I'll try to be a better patient, but I can't promise how good I can be. I've learned that patience isn't one of my virtues."

Maggie brought him some broth and sage tea with honey for him to drink. She also put a chamber pot by the side of his bed. She told him in no uncertain terms that he was to use it, there was no way he was going outside to go to the bathroom.

"Are you going to give me a sponge bath?" Sam asked mischievously. "I might learn to like them with you doing the bathing..."

"Oh, you..." Maggie told him in return. "You laugh now, but Doctor Mitcham had me help operate on you. I didn't know if I could do it, but the good doctor told me I'd better not throw up or pass out on him, because he could only take care of one patient at a time. I told him then and I'm telling you now, I'll do whatever it takes to get you better! So, be prepared!" Maggie left him to finish the broth and sage tea. She knew that it wouldn't be long before he was sleeping again. It was a relief that he had woken up so soon after he was operated on.

Maggie met Cade at the front door and took him into see Sam. Sam was just getting done with the broth. He told Maggie he wanted some steak for dinner. He was sure that eating steak would get him back to normal much faster than drinking colored water!

Maggie just took the dishes from him and left him to talk to Cade.

"Hell, Sam, you scared us to death! Mary and I both lost several years off our lifespan from thinking the worst about you getting shot. Then I find you giving your nurse trouble as soon as I walk in the door!" Cade told his friend. "First, the rabies now a robbery and a stampede. What in heaven's name is going to happen next?"

"I'm hoping nothing! Although I do want to get the money back for the banks. Did you know Jackson Slaughter or Scott Lane?" Sam asked.

"I did, but not well. They've come out to ask if I needed anyone to help out at the ranch, but I was barely keeping the kids and me going, how was I going to pay some cowboys when I didn't have any money to even get us supplies? They seemed nice enough, but you know when you shake hands with someone? When I shook their hands, they weren't calloused like most cowboys and ranchers are. They weren't used to doing much manual labor at all. I didn't know how much help they would have been out at the ranch. Now that my boys are old enough to help, Mary and I do all right by ourselves." Cade explained to the Sheriff.

Maggie stuck her head in the door to let them know she had just gotten a letter from her sister, Brenda, from St. Louis. She wrote to tell them that Wes and Lily Peters were the proud parents of a little girl. She waited a few minutes and then told them, "They've named her Mary Margaret after Mary and me. Imagine someone naming a baby after me...I'm sure not somebody special like Mary is...I'm going to have to get busy and make them something for my namesake." She left them smiling and humming a tune.

Sam disagreed with Maggie and so did Cade. Maggie was very special to all of them. Cade left shortly after talking to Sam. He gave Maggie a hug and told her to get word to them if she needed anything.

Sam called out for Maggie to come in and see him. He had something to get off his chest. He started with, "Maggie, how in heaven's name can you think that you're not something special?!! You are one of those people that are as beautiful on the inside as you are on the outside! You make every one of us feel special from little Andie and cantankerous Reece and myself, to a lost Silas that you've transformed into feeling good about himself. Andie has never known a home...until yours. You've made her and all of us feel like we're home, our home, instead of being boarders. You light up every room you go into with your smiles and laughter. You go through hell to help your friends and protecting everyone around you. I agree that it was an honor that Wes and Lily named their baby after you and Mary, but that baby girl is a very lucky little girl to have two such special women looking after her. Now I don't want to hear another word that you're not special...or you're unworthy of the honor. I'm here to tell you that you're about the best woman I know or have ever known!" Sam paused, glad he'd spoken up, but a little embarrassed, too. He wasn't sure how Maggie would take what he just said. "Now go back to doing whatever you had been doing..."

Never in all her life had anyone stood up for her like Sam did! She didn't remember anyone holding her in such high esteem as Sam did! She burst out crying and threw herself into Sam's good arm. "Oh, Sam, nobody has ever said such nice things about me in all my life! Thank you...you make me feel very...humble..." Then Maggie wiped her eyes with the back of her hand and kissed Sam on his check. "I'm really glad you're going to be all right Sheriff Kincaid!" Then she turned and almost ran from the room to go back to what she was doing in the kitchen. Sam just smiled, he was glad he had told Maggie what he had been thinking. It was something she needed to hear. He was a little angry that her no-account husband had never told her anything to make her feel worthwhile. If he could, he'd shoot him all over again for all the grief he had caused her over the years. It was a damn waste of a good woman!

Maggie was run ragged for the next two weeks caring for Sam. She did manage to keep her garden under control with the help of Andie and Silas. She did manage to make the dresses, butter, and eggs to help pay off her debt to Jonah Clark. But she did not get much sleep. For one thing, it wasn't as comfortable as her bed. While it was fine to sit in and sew, it was too hard to lie down and try to get some sleep at night. She was sleeping with one eye open to make sure that Sam didn't need anything and that didn't help either!

Andie was taking advantage of the situation and using every excuse she could come up with to spend time with her Uncle. She brought him some of Maggie's books and begged him to read to her. She brought in Paddy and Minnie to play on the bed and on the floor with her. She even took some of the embroidery that Maggie was teaching her into Sam's room to sew while she talked to him. Sam loved spending time with Andie, but he wasn't any good at trying to help her sew! He hugged her every chance he got, and he also tickled her to make her laugh. Andie loved it. Andie hated that her Uncle had gotten shot, but she loved being able to spend so much time with the Uncle she loved so much.

Reece wasn't having any luck at finding Slaughter or his accomplice. He had heard nothing from any of the towns in the area. Nor had there been any sightings from the townspeople in Pine City. He had disappeared off the face of the earth or at least Wyoming! He talked to Sam several times a day keeping him appraised of what he was doing and how little he had found out about Slaughter or his cohorts. He was feeling very disheartened and couldn't wait for Sam to be in a position to work again as his partner. And then to make things worse, Maggie got a new boarder. She was going to be the new school teacher. Her name was Tessa Madison.

She was like no school teacher that Reece had ever met. To begin with, she was a lot older than they usually were. Some people called her an old maid, but Reece thought she was way too pretty to be an old maid. She was probably about thirty or maybe even thirty-five. She told them she had been teaching for almost twenty years. She had left her teaching job in Garrison, Wyoming because she had been there too long. One of her ex-students had come back and was going to marry another of her ex-student's. She had her teaching certificate and it would be a perfect situation if she could teach until they started a family. Tessa felt like she needed to go somewhere new and start over. She heard about the teaching position in Pine City and decided that she would make the move.

After having been teaching for almost twenty years, she was more than capable to teach in Pine City. But school marms were supposed to be fat and ugly to Reece's way of thinking. Tessa was anything but fat and far from ugly! She had blonde hair that curled about her face even though it was in a neat bun on top of her head. She was about average height, but she seemed taller because she carried herself with grace and confidence. She had sparkling green eyes and freckles across her nose. Reece had always been partial to freckles. He didn't know how he would fare living across the woman in Maggie's house.

Maggie and Andie fell in love with Tessa. Andie said she wouldn't mind going to school if Tessa were her teacher. Tessa put her things away and rolled up her sleeves and dug in helping Maggie and Andie pull weeds in her garden. She didn't treat Silas any different from anyone else. It didn't take longer than an afternoon for Tessa to feel at home. Maggie and Andie were going to take her over to the schoolhouse tomorrow, so she could start getting ready for the coming school year. Everyone was happy about her coming to the boarding house, except Reece.

He found himself tongue-tied around her. He was spending more time combing his hair in the morning instead of just putting on his hat. He made sure that all his buttons were done up. He made sure that his room was picked up and he started to shave every other day. Reece was in a quandary. He sure liked looking at Tessa, but he didn't like the way she made him feel. He was a confirmed bachelor for God's sake! He wasn't supposed to react to another woman when you were the ripe old age of forty-three!

Fortunately, Reece didn't think that anyone knew how she made him feel. He was pretty good at covering up his feelings, or so he thought, until Sam started teasing him about her when he stopped in to report on the day's happenings.

"That Tessa sure is a good-looking woman. Pine City is lucky to find such an experienced teacher for their children." Sam told him with a twinkle in his eyes. "If I didn't like Maggie so much, I might try spending some time with her to get to know her a little more..."

Reece glanced up and turned red under his collar. "Do whatever you want to do, it won't make no difference to me. But Maggie is sure something special, I wouldn't like for you to make a mistake and let her go. She's the perfect mother for little Andie, and I can see sparks fly every time you get near her." Reece mumbled.

"I feel sparks whenever I'm near her. I like how she makes me feel. Don't worry, I'm not going to let Maggie go. I'm just taking things slow and easy. She had a real rough time with her last husband, I don't want to rush her. I want it to be right for both of us, or maybe I should say all three of us! I don't think Andie would ever forgive me if I chased Maggie away from making us a family! She's been not too subtle dropping hints about making Maggie her real mother one of these days!" Sam laughed at the relieved look on Reece's face that he wasn't going to go after Tessa. But he wasn't done getting a rise out of his friend, "Just you wait till the men of this town get a look at Tessa, they'll be a long line just waiting to take her to dinner or to take her on a stroll some summer night..."

He let it drop, he just wanted to plant a seed in his mind. He'd love for Reece to find someone to spend the rest of his life with. He didn't want him to become a lonely old man wishing things had been different in his life. But he knew how he felt, he'd been pole-axed with his feelings for Maggie! He thought he was a confirmed bachelor, but she had put thoughts into his mind of what could be. Images of Maggie holding Cade and Mary's little boy came to his mind. He would love to see Maggie holding their son or daughter someday. He would love to help her fulfill her dream of filling this house with children in the not too distant future. He didn't know if he loved Maggie, but he sure spent a lot of time thinking about her. It was her face he saw in his dreams, and it was her opinion he sought about matters that came up. He sure cared an awful lot about her but never having been in love before, he didn't have anything to compare it to. It seemed that both Reece and he were in for some long days and nights!

CHAPTER 17

After two weeks, the doctor finally gave Sam permission to get dressed and to go back to work. Sam missed being home and seeing so much of Andie and Maggie. But he sure liked getting back to work. He and Reece planned a strategy about the robberies. Sam figured that if no one had seen Slaughter, then it must be someone in town helping him hide. They must be getting him medical help and food and taking it somewhere. They had to start looking closer to home for the culprits. Reece thought that the General Store sold everything you would need to help a wounded man and feed him. So, he often positioned himself outside the Clark's store and watched who went in and came out and what they were carrying.

For two long days he saw nothing, but then he watched as Matt Hunt, Michael Hunt's oldest boy, came out of the store carrying a package. He stopped to shove it into his saddle bags, then he casually rode out of town. Considering that he was going in the opposite direction of his home, Reece found that to be extremely interesting. He watched him come back three hours later. Reece told Sam about it. Sam told him to keep watching, but he did go in and asked Jonah what exactly Matt Hunt had bought.

"It's strange that you should ask. I found it mighty interesting that he bought some iodine, bandages, some healing cream, coffee, beef jerky, and some cans of beans. I remember asking him if he was going camping, and he told me that he had a friend that needed some provisions. That was all. He's come in a couple more times and he gets about the same thing every time." Jonah told him.

"Thanks, Jonah! Keep this under your hat but let us know if he gets anything else, will you?" Sam asked him.

"I sure will. That Matthew is a strange one. He's always been a bully. Pushing little kids off the boardwalk, throwing rocks to break a window of anyone who yells at him, now he's taken to wearing a gun and holster. I don't reckon what he'll do next to anyone who gets in his way. Be careful." Jonah warned and then left to help another customer. He called back over his shoulder, "It's sure nice to see you up and around again. You gave us all a scare."

Sam nodded his head that he appreciated the kind words and the information. Could Matthew Hunt be the one who stampeded the cattle? Could it be possible that he helped them rob his own father's bank? He didn't know enough about the members of the town to decide about Matthew. He told Reece to keep watching and left to go talk to Maggie. She had been a member of this community for long enough to hear about individual families. He'd ask for her input on the situation. He also knew that he didn't have to ask her to keep it quiet for now.

Maggie, Andie, Tessa, and Silas were picking green beans from the garden. They had filled several buckets and it looked like she was getting ready to can them. They looked up when he walked into the yard.

"Maggie could I have a word with you? I hate to keep you from your work, but it's important." Sam asked her and winked at Andie.

"Sure, I'll be right there. If you want to keep on working, fine, but I think it would be a good idea if we all took a lemonade and cookie break. How does that sound? You all get something to drink and I'll talk to Sam and see what he wants." Maggie brushed off the dirt on her pants and washed her hands using the pump in the barn. "What's up Sam? Is everything all right? You're not hurt, again are you?"

"I'm fine, Maggie, but I need some information about one of the citizens of this town, and I didn't know who else to ask." He paused a minute and then brushed off the small bit of dirt on Maggie's nose. He couldn't help himself and leaned down and kissed her too. "It's about Matthew Hunt. What can you tell me about him?"

"That little turd!" Maggie shocked Sam with her language and then he burst out laughing. Maggie smiled at Sam's reaction to her slip of the tongue. "He's been into trouble all over town since he's been old enough to walk. His parents have too much money and they buy him out of trouble all the time. He's insulted about every business owner in town, he's taken things from their stores without paying for them. His mama just soothes things over with money. He's been drinking since he was around twelve and pounding on my door since he found out about the opposite sex. I've threatened him with my derringer more than once and had some windows broken for turning him down. I don't know of a single person he's decent to not even his parents. He does what he wants, when he wants, to whom ever he wants to. To his credit Sheriff Tate did throw him in jail a time or two or three. But Michael Hunt would just march down to the jail and pay whatever fine Tate imposed. He is not a nice kid, although, I don't think you could call him a kid anymore. I'd say he's about twenty now. I'm just glad he won't be one of Tessa's students. He's given a lot of teachers' hell over the years until he left school for good several years back. I think his folks made him go to school for so long just to get him out of the house for most of the day! Does that answer your question?" Maggie asked hoping that Sam would kiss her again before he went back to work.

119

Sam was thinking along those lines himself, and he pulled Maggie towards him to kiss her several times before he started back to the office. "Thanks for the information, Maggie, it tells me a lot." He tipped his hat and winked again at Andie and pulled one of her braids as he left. Maggie wondered what that was all about. But knowing Matt Hunt, he was probably in trouble again. He wouldn't find being up against Sam or Reece as easy as Tate had been. She almost wanted to see the mess he'd gotten himself into! With a smile over the kiss, she and the others went back to picking beans. Maggie had a lot to get done before they took Tessa over to her schoolhouse.

Sam's gut told him that he thought that Matt Hunt was the shooter of the stampede. He also felt that he was caring for Jackson Slaughter himself. Now what would be the best way to tackle this problem? They could follow him out of town, but if they were spotted, they'd lose whatever advantage they had. He could lead them on a merry chase through the vast woods that surrounded Pine City. They could lose Slaughter for good and the stolen money.

The town was getting ready for the Fourth of July celebration they held every year. Everyone from miles around planned on spending the day in town for the games, stands, dancing and fireworks. Maybe he and Reece could spend a little time needling Matt Hunt and get him to make a mistake. It was worth thinking about. He and Reece began to plan.

Andie was excited about going up town to the celebration. Maggie told her that she would be able to spend the day playing with Josie, Kit, Cooper, and Cody. She would make a picnic lunch that they could all share. She made sure that Silas would join them, and that Sam and Reece would take a few minutes off from work to join them for lunch. She hoped that she would get to dance with Sam for at least one dance tonight.

Tessa was not indifferent to Reece. She had had her share of boyfriends over the years. But no one ever got to her as his silent presence in the house. He probably hadn't said more than a dozen words to her since she moved in and those were 'Please pass the salt or can I have the meat?" But she found him watching her. She didn't mind Reece's eyes on her, she did her best to look good all the time, but when you're picking green beans or helping to can them, it's hard! Maggie had told her there would be dancing tonight, and Tess hoped that maybe he would ask her to dance, at least once. After all she didn't really know anybody in town other than Sam, Reece, Silas, Andie, Maggie, and Jonah Clark and his wife. Being the mayor, he had the keys to the school house and Maggie took her over to meet them yesterday as they went to the school.

Tess loved the school. It had a very large room with lots of windows that made it look bright and airy. It had been closed up for several months as they planted and got their crops in, but she didn't mind cleaning it to make it look almost new for her students. Maggie had been telling her about some of the students that would be in her classroom this year. She would have a full house that's for sure!

Maggie held tightly to Andie's hand until she spotted the Murphy's up ahead. She leaned down and pressed a dime into Andie's hand and told her to go have fun with Kit and Josie. Andie was thrilled to have money of her own to spend. She gave Maggie a huge hug and took off running. Andie was actually wearing a dress today. She looked really pretty in her purple calico with a nice bow at the waist. Maggie had even tied little purple bows in her braids. She waved to Cade and Mary and took Tessa over to meet her friends.

"Mary let me hold little Charlie! He's growing like a weed! He'll be going to school in no time at this rate!" She told them. "Mary,

Cade, I'd like you to meet Tessa Madison, our new school teacher. Tessa, this is Mary and Cade Murphy. Cade and I have been friends since we were in school, but Mary has only been here for about a year or so. They have six children, three of which will probably be your students. You will find them bright, cheerful, and very helpful. They will not be discipline problems, I promise you!"

"They'd better not be!" Both Mary and Cade said at the same time. Everyone laughed. "It's nice to meet you, Miss Madison. How do you find our little town?" Cade asked while putting his arm around his little wife. Tessa could see they were a very loving couple. That was nice, very nice! She liked to see children that come from loving homes. They were usually well-adjusted kids and not problems in her classroom.

"I love your little town! Maggie and Andie have been wonderful about showing me the town and my schoolhouse. I love her house. I already feel like I've been here for a long time. Would you know that I'm even learning how to pick green beans and can them? I'm having the time of my life in Maggie's garden. I've never had one before, and I love picking the vegetables and eating what we picked!"

Mary laughed. She knew how much the garden meant to every farmer and rancher in the area in keeping their families fed. Having had a garden her entire life, she still loved seeing the tiny seeds sprout and give new life to their dinner menu. She also noticed how happy Maggie seemed. She was at ease with Tessa and Andie, but she saw her looking around the crowd almost as if she were searching for someone.

It was like she conjured him up. Maggie wanted to see Sam, and there he was right beside her squeezing her hand. "Howdy all you Murphy's! Been meeting our new school marm? I think she's going to be a dandy! She won't have any trouble keeping those kids in line." Sam laughed with the rest of them.

That's when a new voice could be heard. "Well, look at that! It looks like Maggie is getting new blood at her boarding house...With two of them there, maybe she'll change it to Maggie's Pleasure House instead! That should keep all of us horny men happy! What the heck?" This was from him as he flew through the air and landed in a fresh pile of horse droppings. "What was that for?"

Reece spoke loud enough for Matthew Hunt to hear him, "That was for showing no respect to the ladies' present. If I hear any more out of you, I'm throwing you in jail." The sparks flying out of Reece's eyes spoke volumes.

But Matthew Hunt wasn't the brightest bully there, "You don't like anyone saying the truth about the...women...in your boarding house. Maybe it's because you and the Sheriff are getting laid by them while the rest of us get shut out!" He yelled to make sure everyone heard him. And then he did something incredibly stupid. He reached for his gun. Before his hand had rested on the butt of his revolver, Reece and Sam both had their guns out and leveled at the young hot-head.

"You better be sure before you even touch that gun, that if you do, it'll be the last thing you ever do." Sam told him in a low voice. "Now this is a town gathering, a friendly town gathering. I don't want to see or hear any more insults not by you or anyone else in this town. If I do, I'm coming looking for you and I'll lock you up in my jail and throw away the key. Do you understand me?"

"Sure, I hear you. But you probably won't have any more luck finding me than you have the bank robbers you went looking for! Fine lot of lawmen we got! You two can't find the bottom of a wet paper bag much less a young kid and bank robbers!" He pulled himself into a standing position and tried to wipe the manure off his boots and pants. "If you'll excuse me, I'm going home to change into clean clothes." With those parting words, he stomped through the crowd towards home. Sam nodded at Reece and then

Reece looked at Tessa and tipped his hat. He took off following an angry Matt Hunt.

"Sorry about that, I hope it didn't put a blight on your celebration." Sam asked quietly to Maggie and Tessa.

"I appreciate you and Reece stepping in and protecting our reputations, such that they are." Maggie told him in little less than a whisper.

"There's nothing wrong with your reputations, Maggie. No one that knows you thinks that you are that kind of woman. Just because that dumb kid said it, doesn't make it true. We know it, and you know it. Let it go and continue to have a good time. All right?" Sam gave her hand another squeeze, "Now I expect that all you lovely ladies will save a dance for me later on tonight."

"Get your own woman, Sam!" Cade told him by hitting him gently in the shoulder, "Mary's taken and I'm not sharing her with anyone!"

"I'm working on it!" Sam told him and hit him back as he walked away following in Reece's wake.

The rest of the day was uneventful, unless you count the fact that Andie caught a greased pig and gleefully pulled it home with a rope. She told them that Porky would be getting a new friend, that is until we fatten them up to eat them!

CHAPTER 18

By evening, the heat of the day had eased. They even had a cool breeze sweep over the land. Lanterns had been hung around the dance floor and the band was tuning up. Most had finished eating their evening meal and now gathered around the dance floor for the music to start. Maggie, Andie, and Tessa were no exception. They were all seated around one of the tables talking with the Murphy family and Jonah and Olivia Clark. Malachi and Elizabeth Graham and Mitch and Ava Drew had already headed back home. Morning comes early when you live on a ranch. They knew they needed to get home to put the children to bed, so they would be ready to get up bright and early tomorrow morning.

Maggie hadn't seen Sam or Reece since the altercation with Matthew Hunt. Much to Maggie's surprise, the incident hadn't been repeated by anyone else in town. Maggie was content just to sit and listen to the music. This was the first time in over nine years that she actually attended the evening festivities. She had always felt lonely watching all the couples dancing with their wives and husbands. She didn't feel comfortable dancing with anyone other than her husband, and she wouldn't let him touch her! It was best just to stay away. But tonight, she felt drawn to the music and spending time with her friends. She almost felt like she belonged like everyone else.

Maggie tapped her foot to the music. She loved to dance, not just line dancing or square dances, but the waltz as well. Suddenly there was a tap on her shoulder, "Ma'am, would you do me the honor of dancing with me?" The voice was low and extremely masculine. Maggie looked over her shoulder and stared right into the dancing eyes of Sam's.

"Why, I would be delighted to join you in a dance!" Maggie told him with a smile. Sam took her out to the dance floor and swept her up in his arms. Maggie felt like they were the only couple dancing. She loved being held by Sam. He was so solid and dependable. Maggie thought she could stay in his arms forever if given the chance.

Sam was enjoying it too. To him, Maggie was the prettiest woman there. She had considerable competition, but she beat them hands down! She was soft as a woman was supposed to be, but strong like a man wants his woman to be. He knew that she would always cover his back. She was someone he could count on and he loved how she made him and everyone else feel. She was special, this woman in his arms. He wondered how he was going to let her know how he felt. In the meantime, he was going to enjoy every minute of being able to hold her in his arms.

Reece wasn't going to let this opportunity go by without holding Tessa at least for one dance. His hands were sweaty, he felt like he had a frog in his throat, he was having trouble getting a full breath, and he felt like he had run several miles. With all that going through his mind, he stepped up in front of Tessa. Reece was a man of few words, "Dance?" He asked.

Tessa smiled and put her hand in his. "Yes." She replied, not sure she could answer him in any more words. He seemed to take the breath right out of her just pulling her into his strong arms. She could feel his breath on her cheek and shivers went up and down her spine. He could feel her tremble in his arms. He knew then that she wasn't oblivious to him either. He pulled her a little closer and she didn't object. Reece's heart was hammering, and he thought it was loud enough for the entire town to hear. Neither party said another word. Neither party wanted the dance to ever end.

It wasn't until they were playing the last few notes of the dance that someone shouted, "FIRE!!" and pointed towards the middle of town. Everyone looked and gasped! The flames showed up bright orange and yellow into the night sky.

Sam was the first to react, "Oh my god! Maggie, I think that's your house!" Everyone took off running toward her home.

It wasn't her house, but it was her barn. Silas lay in a crumpled mass on the ground where he had been overpowered by whoever set the fire. Sam ran into the burning pyre to help get the horses and cow out while they still could. Maggie and Tessa helped take Silas into the house and she asked someone to go get the Doctor. Cade and Jonah were chasing her chickens out of the barn and into crates that had once housed them before they were turned into their nests. Another man was dragging Porky and Andie's new 'greased' pig away from the towering inferno.

They saw Beauty come running out of the barn and Reece's horse. Reece went in to see if he could help Sam when he finally came out leading the bawling cow and a very frightened Beast! All the straw that had been delivered to the loft didn't help them keep the fire under control. A bucket brigade was formed from the well to the barn and strong arms took the full buckets and tossed it on the blaze. Others were wetting down her house and smoke house to keep the fire from spreading. Andie sat huddled on the porch with the rest of the Murphy and Clark children. The fire reminded her so much of the night her other boarding house burned, and she lost her father. She wouldn't stop crying until she saw her uncle come out of the barn and then she tried to run to him, but the caring hands of the Murphy children held her back. "He's all right, Andie. Let him work with the others to get the fire out. Stay here, where he'll know you're safe." Chris told her. He put his arm around her, he would protect her just like his little sister. Andie leaned against him as much for support as comfort.

The Doctor was checking Silas over carefully. Someone had hit him over the head with something very hard. His guess was the butt end of a revolver. Silas needed several stitches and it took a while to clean up the wound and get it wrapped. Silas didn't wake up until he was almost done. He stared into the caring eyes of the doctor and felt someone holding onto his hand. He could hear someone crying. It took Silas several minutes to figure out why he was lying down and what had happened.

"I got to get to Miz Maggie!" Silas told them and tried to get up.

"You're not going anywhere!" The doctor told him in no uncertain terms. "And Maggie is right here holding your hand. Now stay still, I'm almost done taking care of the stitches in your head."

Silas turned his head slightly to see Maggie sitting beside him holding his hand and crying. "Oh, Silas, I thought we had lost you! I was so scared. Please just lay quiet so the doctor can make you better..." Maggie sobbed.

"Don't cry...Miz Maggie...I don't think I can stand for you to be sad...Nobody's cared about me for more years than I can remember..." Silas paused and wiped his nose and his eyes with the hand not being held by Maggie. "I tried to stop him...he wanted to burn down your house...But I knocked him down and turned around to put out the torch, and that's when he must have knocked me out...Is your house all right? I smell smoke..." Silas closed his eyes and thought the worst.

"You saved the house, Silas. It's the barn that's burning. All that straw that we bought thinking we were doing the smart thing...you and I both know that the barn was so old and dry, it wouldn't take much to get a fire started and to burn it down. But the important thing is that, all the animals got out safe and sound, even Paddy and Minnie, and no one was seriously hurt. The Murphy kids found Andie's pets huddled against the house on the back porch and gave them to Andie. She's holding onto them with both hands and arms...It's all right, Silas...People are more important than any old barn...We'll rebuild as soon as we get the money. We'll be all right, you'll see." Maggie told him and then leaned down to hug the little man who had come to mean an awful lot to her over the course of the last few weeks.

It took the men of the town several hours to make sure that the fire was completely out and couldn't be spread to the rest of the town or to the house. They were exhausted, and soot covered their faces, arms, and clothes. Maggie thanked them for all their efforts. They told her that they would be back to clean up the debris and help her build another one. All she would need would be lumber, and Mr. Williams of the lumber yard told her he would sell to her at cost. Just let him know when she would be starting the barn raising.

Maggie was humbled by all their help and support. It was late, and the Murphy's still had to travel the distance to get their crew home. Maggie offered to let them stay in her house, but Cade and Mary told her they had livestock to see to, not to mention that they were running out of clean diapers for little Charlie! Mary told her the children could sleep in the wagon on the way home and then climb into their own beds to sleep whatever was left of the night away. They both kissed her on the cheek and gave her a hug as they left.

The horses and cow had been hobbled in the grass behind the corral and a temporary pen had been built to keep the pigs from running away. The chickens would be fine in the crates until morning. Sam and Reece sat on the back porch drinking coffee and talking about what they were going to do.

"First thing in the morning, I'm going over and arrest that son-of-a-bitch who started this fire!" Reece told him in a near shout. "You and I both know who did this because we had a little set-to in town! I'm going to nail Hunt's butt to the wall!"

"Yes, we are. We're also going to make sure that his parents foot the bill for building Maggie a new barn. They've been paying his way out of trouble for years, we're not going to stop that tradition just because we're going to see their son going to the territory prison! Once he sees that we're not going to let him off this time, maybe he'll tell us where to find Slaughter and the money. Either way, he's going to pay." Sam told him.

They cleaned up and met Maggie and Tessa at the kitchen table. Andie lay across Maggie's lap and the next chair. Paddy and Minnie were asleep in a box in the corner of the kitchen. Maggie's eyes were red from crying, but her hands were steady as she reached up to grab Sam's hand as he came close. "Thank you for going in to save the animals, but Sam, so help me god! If you ever do anything to endanger your life again, I'll kill you myself with my own two hands...I have never been so scared than to see you disappear in that fiery inferno...You risked your life over a couple of horses and a cow! Don't you know how much we love you? Andie and I couldn't live with knowing that you were gone..." Her voice trailed away as she realized what she had just told Sam. She hoped that he was too tired to realize that she had just told him that she loved him!

Sam was tired, but not that tired. He bent over and kissed Maggie several times and then whispered, "I love you too Maggie! You couldn't get rid of me even if you tried!" Maggie was so happy she didn't even care that Reece and Tessa were with them in the room. She threw her arms around Sam and kissed him soundly back.

For such a terrible end to a lovely day, Maggie was happy all over again!

CHAPTER 19

Sam and Reece did indeed get cleaned up and then Sam carried Andie up to her own bed to sleep. When he came down, Maggie was starting on their breakfast. She knew they were going out to get whoever had set the fire, but they weren't going out on an empty stomach! She had eggs, bacon, toast and fried potatoes on the table even before they could object.

Maggie looked them both in the eye and simply said, "Sit! I know you're going out to get the man responsible for all this. I understand, but you're not going out on an empty stomach, it's probably going to be a very long day for both of you and after getting no sleep at all last night, you can't keep going on good intentions. Now eat, while I make you up some sandwiches in case you get hungry later on." She worked while they ate. "You're both too important to lose over a stupid 'ole barn. I can stand to lose the barn, but I couldn't stand it if something happened to either of you. So where ever you go, watch each other's backs and heaven help you if you get hurt! I'll be all over you to give you hell for getting hurt!"

As Sam finished, he went over and drew Maggie to him for a hug and a kiss. This was his woman! He'd be coming back to her come hell or high water. "I love you, Maggie." Sam whispered in her ear, "We have a lot to talk about when I get home tonight!"

This time Maggie kissed Sam and told him, "I love you, too, Sam! Be careful!"

Both men walked out the door a few minutes later. Maggie gathered up all the smoky and soot filled clothes and started washing clothes. She didn't think she could sleep even if she were to permit herself to lie down. She had too much to think about. Sam loved her! And how was she going to be able to afford to build a new barn? Where was she going to keep her animals until she obtained shelter for them? Too many questions and not enough answers!

Sam and Reece were both armed and ready to confront Matthew Hunt. They knew he was probably sleeping this early in the morning. He didn't think they were smart enough to figure out that he was the one responsible for the fire. He also didn't know that Silas was still alive and would be able to identify him. They hoped to catch him totally unaware and unprepared.

Sam knocked on the front door and Reece went around to the back, just in case he tried to escape.

"Who in the devil is knocking at the door this early in the morning?" Michael Hunt came to the door wearing only his long john's. "What's so important that it couldn't wait until a decent hour of the day to come calling?"

"I want to talk to your son, Matthew." Sam began watching the faces of both Michael and his wife, Marissa, who had joined him in her wrapper. "We have reason to believe that he set fire to Maggie McDonald's barn last night and attacked a man in the process."

"What...he couldn't have done this!" Marissa Hunt cried out. "Michael do something, don't let them take my baby!

"Mrs. Hunt, we have an eye witness. Plus, I think we'll find the smell of kerosene on his clothes of last night. I'm afraid he's responsible for the barn, supplies, straw, and tools that were lost in the fire. And then there's the attempted murder of the man who works for Maggie. Your son is going away for a long time." Sam told them. He also caught a glimpse of his deputy coming around the corner of the house. He had Matthew handcuffed in front of him. Matthew wasn't happy and couldn't believe these clod-hoppers had him handcuffed like a common criminal.

"Pa! Do something! I don't want to be locked up in their lousy jail!" Matthew whined.

"Mathew! Did you do this terrible thing?" Michael asked, but even from standing ten feet away, the smell of kerosene could be detected.

"Of course not, Pa! They're trying to railroad me for calling Maggie a few names, nothing bad, I promise you." Matt continued to whine and to lie.

Reece grabbed the front of his shirt and picked him up and shook him. "Do you call yelling that Maggie was opening up a Pleasure Palace nothing bad? Plus, I believe you called them whores!"

"My son would never use that kind of language around ladies!" Marissa argued. "He's a gentleman like his father. All my children are perfectly mannered, just...high strung. Sometimes Matthew has done some childish pranks, like all boys do. It's not bad enough to get arrested for!"

"Well I disagree, Mrs. Hunt. Setting fire to a barn that could have spread to half the town is not a childish prank. Hitting someone over the head causing them to have a concussion and several stitches is not a childish prank. And helping his friends rob your bank is not a childish prank." Sam let those words drop like a bombshell into the conversation. He was watching the reactions of both Matthew and his father.

Matthew was astonished that these two bozos could have figured out that he was the third man in the robbery. How did they link him to Slaughter and Lane? How was he going to get out of this? He did not want to go to prison!!

Michael couldn't believe what he had just heard! But then his son had been acting strangely, at least more strangely than usual. He was gone for long periods of time. He was riding that horse of his all over the place. He was always short tempered and didn't want to talk to anyone. And then there was the money. He seemed to have plenty of cash to spend at the saloons and on gambling and whores. Where did that money come from? When realization came to him, he reached for his son. He shook him until his teeth rattled, "You miserable son-of-a-bitch! You stole from your own father? How could you?!!"

Matthew couldn't believe that his father turned on him. He answered with a sneer, "Why wouldn't I? You're the only person in Pine City that has any money! If I'm going to rob somebody, it's going to be worth my while. They're going to be someone who's rich!"

At that point, Michael stuck his son with a right punch in the jaw. Matthew went down with blood trickling down from his mouth. "Take him to jail and let him rot for all I care!" Michael shouted.

Reece smiled, "With pleasure. Come on jack-ass. I hope you like bread and water, because that's all you'll be getting until I get over everything you've done. It might take a while. Oh, and by the way the territorial judge will be in to see you in two days. They call him Hanging Judge Sanders. We just might get to have a hanging here in Pine City. Something I know you'll look forward to. Now march, I'm not going to carry you to jail. I might drag your ass, but I'm sure not making this easy on you!" He pulled him up by his shirt. And wonder of wonders, Matthew started walking to jail. This wasn't turning out like he thought it would at all!

Sam wasn't done with the Hunts. "Mr. Hunt, I expect you to make arrangements for the rebuilding of Maggie's barn and for housing her animals until its done. Not only do you have to build that barn, you will need to duplicate all the tools, wheelbarrows, and the buggy she recently purchased, and it was burned with the barn last night. If your son doesn't cooperate and tell us where

Slaughter and the money are hidden, I wouldn't be surprised to see him going away for the rest of his life to the territorial prison in Carson City. If he cooperates, he might get out sooner. But he'll still be an old man. I'll expect you in later today to tell me the arrangements about the barn." Sam tipped his hat and walked away, he could hear Marissa arguing with her husband about their son. He was afraid there were no easy answers about what was going to happen to him.

Matthew was not being cooperative. Reece had stripped him down to his long johns to search him for any hidden weapons. He had found a knife in his boot and a small derringer in the pocket of his coat. He was using some very colorful language about the methods that Reece was using. Reece just kept laughing, especially when Matthew told him he was a respected member of the community and the town wouldn't let him be treated this way! "Listen to me, Hunt! After what you've done, nobody in this town cares what happens to you! You've stepped on too many toes to get away with any of this! Mama and Papa can't buy your way out of this. Get comfortable, you're going to be spending some time in this jail and in particular in this jail cell. You can yell all you want, but Sam and I will just shut the door so that we don't have to listen to you." With that Reece threw his now searched clothes back into the jail cell with him and slammed the door connecting the cells to the Sheriff's office. Sam was sitting at his desk smiling. They both felt good about putting at least one of the robbers behind jail. Now they just had to wait until Matthew got chatty. They didn't think it would take long. Matthew was not used to not getting his way or of being thrown into a twelve by twelve cell. He had a bucket of water to drink and another bucket to use as his toilet. There was also a cot, only this cot was nailed to the floor and to the wall. It wasn't going anywhere. There wasn't even a breeze coming through the steel bars on the window. Matthew sat down on the cot and put his head in his hands. He would not stand for this kind of treatment, not from the likes of them or from anybody. He had to think of a way out of here!

Michael Hunt and his wife had a busy morning. Michael arranged with the lumber yard to start building Maggie's barn today, just as soon as they cleared away all the rubble from the fire. He also made arrangements for her animals to be housed in the livery. Her eggs would be delivered daily to her house, and the milk would be delivered twice daily. He talked to the livery owner about what kind of buggy she had purchased and arranged for a duplicate to be sent to her house immediately.

Marissa went to see their lawyer. She wanted to know what could be done for her boy. She couldn't and wouldn't let him hang! After hearing the facts, Eli Peterson told her that unless he told them where to find the money and the other robber, her precious son didn't have a chance in hell of getting out of this. That's when Marissa headed toward the jail. She wanted to see what kind of treatment her son was receiving. She was also going to order him to tell the Sheriff and Deputy what they wanted to hear. If it meant saving her son from hanging, prison didn't sound quite so bad. At least he would be alive!

Matthew was so glad to see his mother! He was starved and hoped she was coming to bring him food or to get him out. But she brought neither food nor good news. She told him exactly what the lawyer had told her. He had to tell them exactly where that other robber was hiding and where the money was. Until they had him and the money, the lawyer told her that he'd have no leniency. So, start talking, she would have no son of hers hanging from the middle of town like a common criminal!

Marissa called in Sam and Reece. "Tell them, Matthew." She ordered her son.

"He and the money are hidden in a cave on the back of Malachi Graham's place. It's close to the river. Slaughter is in a bad way. His gun shots aren't healing very well. They may be infected..." Matthew told them with a whiny voice. "I ain't no doctor you know! I did the best I could. This wasn't supposed to be so complicated! We were just going to all go away and see the world, have some adventures! Some adventure this is!" He ended up pouting in the corner.

"Reece and I will see if what you say if the truth, Matthew. If it is, we'll be sure to tell Judge Sanders that you told us where to find the other robber. I doubt you'll hang, but I don't see any way out of doing time in prison." They made sure that Marissa Hunt left the Sheriff's Office with them, they didn't think she was above letting her son out of prison and giving him some money to make a run for it. Sam made sure the office was locked and took off to find their horses.

It took them over an hour to get to the river behind Graham's house. It took almost another hour to find the correct cave where Slaughter was hiding. He looked like he was already dead. But he moaned when Sam picked him up and slung him over his shoulder. They tied him down on his horse and loaded up the money in the bags. Their first stop would be to the doctors to see if the patient would live. Then they would return the stolen money. They would need for Hunt to confirm that all the money was there or at least most of it. Matthew had been spending a lot of it on gambling, liquor, and whores.

Slaughter's chances weren't good. Gangrene had set in and there were red streaks running up his leg. Slaughter would lose his leg, Doctor Mitcham hoped he could save his life. But he wasn't making any promises. The good Doc set to work immediately on saving the no-account robbers life. He wanted him alive to spend the rest of his life in prison where he belonged. Dying was just too easy for all that he had done to the town. He needed to suffer.

Maggie was shocked when she saw men return to her home the next morning. Even more surprised to learn that banker Michael Hunt was paying for the lumber and labor to get her a new barn. Silas was thrilled that Maggie wouldn't be hurt any more by the fire. He knew she was lean on money and knew that she didn't know where she would get enough to build another one, even with the town's help. To Silas's way of thinking, justice was being served. Maggie wouldn't let him get out of bed until he had been cleared by the doctor. He promised that he would come over later today to check on his patient. She was waiting on him like he was somebody special. He loved Maggie for how well she took care of him. Andie come in and let him hold her kitten and puppy and told him everything that was happening outside. She felt important that she got to tell someone something they didn't already know.

Tessa and Maggie started on canning the corn today just to stay busy. They were both thinking of the safety of Reece and Sam and wondering if things were going as well as they hoped they would. Canning corn would keep them busy and it had to be done. Even after catastrophes, there was still work that had to be finished. Maggie appreciated the livery man coming down to pick up her chickens and to give her eggs and milk while the barn was being done. He told her to think nothing of it, that Mister Hunt was paying for it all. He also told her that her new buggy would be delivered when the barn was ready. Maggie couldn't believe it! How had Sam gotten Michael Hunt to do any of this? The man was a miracle worker that's for sure!

CHAPTER 20

It was Doctor Mitcham who told Maggie about the other robber. As soon as he was done with surgery, they transferred Slaughter to the jail. He was put in the cell next to Matthew Hunt. The doctor thought he would live to spend the rest of his life in prison. He was pretty thorough in checking Silas over. But he had to admit that the little man looked pretty good. He wasn't seeing double any more, and he told the doctor that the headache wasn't so bad that he couldn't get out of bed.

Doctor Mitcham just laughed, "It's because you've got such a hard head and are too stubborn to stay down! You take it easy, you can help in building another barn, chicken coup, and pig pen, but you have to go slow. I don't want a relapse! Are you listening to me, Silas? I'll sic Maggie on you if you overdo it!"

"You can bet your boots that I'll keep an eye on him, Doc! I couldn't bear to lose my best employee." Maggie shook her finger at Silas with laughter in her voice. "He'll listen to me or he won't get any more desserts!"

"I'll do whatever Miz Maggie tells me to do, Doc. She's the best cook around and I ain't going to miss out on getting them." Silas smiled at Maggie. They were both glad he was on the mend and no serious harm was done.

"Doc, would you like to stay for dinner? We've got plenty...I'm used to making a lot, because Reece and Sam eat like there's no tomorrow!" Maggie asked him.

"I'd love to, Maggie, but I've still got to go check out my patient over at the jail and then go home to clean up after the surgery I did today to save his life. I don't dare put it off any longer. Are you sure that you won't give all this up and become my nurse?" Doc told her as he packed up his medical bag to leave.

"Sorry, Doc, I'm very happy here, but I will volunteer to come over and help clean up your offices whenever you need my help. Now that I know that the sight won't make me throw up or pass out, I think I could help clean up the mess you make from your patients. Do you need my help?" Maggie offered out of the goodness of her heart, but she was also thinking that this could be another way to add a little income to her already strapped budget.

"Maggie you're hired! How about you come over once a week to clean the office and my living rooms behind the office? I'll pay you for cleaning and doing my laundry. If I have any extra operations, I'll send word over to come for an extra day and extra pay. How does that sound?" He inquired. He liked how she didn't shy away from work or unpleasant experiences.

"I'll be over tomorrow afternoon if that's a good time to come. I'll be washing here and canning from the garden in the morning. If you put some meat on the counter, I'll start a soup or stew while I'm there, and then all you'll have to do when you get hungry is go in and heat it up." Maggie told him feeling happy about the extra money coming into the budget.

"Sounds like a plan, Maggie. I'll go over to the General Store now to get the ingredients for stew and biscuits. I can already taste them!" Doc left them smiling.

Maggie let Silas get up and sit on the porch and watch them clear away all the debris from the fire. They had certainly been productive. Most of the burned mound had already been removed. Another couple of loads in their wagons should see it done. They wanted to start tomorrow on the new barn. Mr. Williams from the lumber yard was sending over ten workers to get it done and get it done quickly. Since Mr. Hunt had told them to get it built in a hurry, he was going to make sure that it got done lickety-split! He was glad that Maggie was getting her barn and it wasn't costing her a penny.

Jonah Clark at the General Store was making a list like Hunt had told him to do of all the tools and supplies that Maggie must have had in her barn. He was replacing them with new ones and wanted them delivered to her house by tomorrow at the latest. Jonah put on the list everything that he could think of, but he was going to ask Silas and Maggie if she had anything else to add. He was very glad that the robbers had been caught, the money recovered, and that Matthew was finally going to have to pay for his part in this entire escapade. As far as he was concerned, he thought that Reece and Sam had gotten him off easy considering what could have happened to the town. He wouldn't gouge Michael Hunt, but he wasn't going to go easy on him either! He had been paying for his son to get off his entire life but not this time.

Sam and Reece were tired. They had been up all night with the dance, fire, arresting both Hunt and Slaughter, and getting justice for Maggie. They felt good about what they had accomplished, but they were bone tired just the same. Hunt had finally stopped yelling and cussing when they brought Slaughter into the cell next to his. He couldn't get over the fact that he had lost a leg because of his ineptitude. Slaughter had a temper, he was going to unleash it on Hunt because he would blame him for not doing a better job getting the bullet out of his leg. He was sure glad they were in two different cells.

Sam couldn't wait to see Maggie tonight. And at the same time, he didn't know what he was going to say to her. He had never been in love before or asked anyone to marry him before. How exactly did you go about such a task? He didn't want to bungle it, he wanted it to be something Maggie would remember for the rest of her life. She had so few precious memories from her first marriage,

Sam wanted to make this one much better. He didn't know what kind of husband he would be, but he was bound and determined that he would be better than her first one!

Reece was also thinking about Tessa. He sure liked dancing with her last night, and he thought she liked it too. He was hoping that if she wasn't too tired, that she might like to take a walk-through town with him. He wanted to ask her permission to court her. He had never courted anyone before, but after all they had been through with the fire and all. He wasn't going to take the chance that Tessa would get away from him. He had been waiting for her his whole life. He didn't want to blow it!

Maggie and Tessa and Andie had spent the day cleaning the soot off everything they could see. It had been tracked into the house and appeared to be on every piece of clothing that anyone wore yesterday. The porches were covered in black soot and the back wall of the house as well. The smoke house didn't seem any worse for the soot or the smoke. Tessa and Andie had helped Maggie scrub the porch and the back wall of the house. This was after they had canned over twenty quarts of corn and green beans. While they were scrubbing, Maggie kept stopping to change out quart jars from the boiling water on the wash stand. Their arms felt like lead by the time they were done. But it sure looked a lot better!

Maggie had put in a venison roast at noon. She had added potatoes and carrots at around three o'clock. All she had to do was slice up the bread she had also started and finished while she was washing out all the dirty clothes. She was exhausted but exhilarated about getting a new barn and cleaning up the mess. She was on tender hooks waiting to see Sam again, but also afraid to see him. What if he had changed his mind about loving her? Her first husband had, what if Sam did too? Before Sam came home, she needed to clean herself up. She knew that she probably looked at bedraggled as she felt!

Sam and Reece came home just as Maggie was pulling dinner out of the oven. Andie was setting the table and Tessa was cutting slices of fresh bread. Silas, they were glad to see, was sitting in one of the rockers in front of the fireplace. His head was still bandaged, but he was smiling as he watched the busy women at work.

It seems that Tessa was telling the kinds of things they would be doing in school. "We'll learn some songs, Andie. One of them will be the 'Star Spangled Banner' which is our national anthem. Every citizen should know that song. We'll go on nature hikes collecting different kinds of grasses and plants that are indigenous to this area. It will be good that the students will be able to identify all of them, and also helpful if they can tell poison ivy from other plants! We'll have spelling bees and Math competitions. You'll be able to play all sorts of games at lunchtime with the other children. I think you'll love being with the other students and as smart as you are, I also think you'll love the challenge of learning. At least that's my plan!" Tess laughed and then she looked up and saw Reece. When he smiled at her, she gave him a huge smile in return.

"Sounds a lot better than when I went to school, Andie! I had this mean, old hag that made us write on the blackboard hundreds of times over and over again if we made a mistake. She also had this board she used on anyone who misbehaved! Boy did that board hurt! I still remember the pain to this day. You've got a lot prettier teacher than ours was too." He blushed as he finally gave Tessa a compliment.

"Thank you, Reece. Just exactly what did you do to get her to use that board on you?" Tessa asked him sweetly.

"Oh, nothing much, just little things." Reece told them looking a little embarrassed about talking about his childhood.

"Uh...huh..." Tessa told him. She knew there was more to this story than he was telling them, but she was willing to let it slide this time. She knew that she would get the whole store one of these days.

Sam walked in and wiped his feet and searched the room until he found Maggie. He breathed a big sigh of relief. The tiredness of the day seemed to flow from his body and be replaced by a feeling of well-being. He sure liked the way she looked and smelled. He walked over and without stopping to think, he pulled her to him and kissed her several times. Wonder of wonders, she kissed him back and held onto him. Andie's mouth dropped open at this turn of events and then she smiled. Maybe she was going to get her wish of having Maggie for her mother after all!

They all sat down to dinner happy that they were all there safe and sound. Maggie listened in awe of their talk with Michael Hunt that he was responsible for building and replacing all she had lost in the fire that his son set.

"I saw that the debris had been removed and I also saw the stacks of lumber that had been delivered. It looks like Michael Hunt is doing what he should be doing. It shouldn't take more than a week or two at the most to get it up and better than it was before. You should make a list of everything you had in the barn, Maggie. That all has to be replaced as well. Maybe Silas could help with that since he was in the barn so much. Did you tell the men building the barn how many stalls to make and to leave room for half of the chicken coup inside the barn? It would probably be a good idea to also make it big enough to put your buggy inside during bad weather. It will stay in good shape longer." Sam told them.

"I ain't no good with writing things down, Sheriff Sam, but if Miz Maggie will write down what I do remember, I'll be glad to tell her all we had in the barn. I'll be needin' some tools to continue to help in the garden and to take care of the animals. Did your saddles get destroyed in the fire?" Silas asked them.

"They did, we'll add them to the list. The livery man was kind enough to loan us some today when we had to go pick up Slaughter. Reece complained the entire way. His wasn't big enough for him, so we might have to order one to his liking. Add saddles to the list and bridles and curry combs and horse blankets, if I can think of anything else, I'll be sure to let you know. But I will tell you this, nothing was lost in the fire that can't be replaced. If someone had lost their lives to that fire, I would feel a whole lot different about it and the justice that awaits Matthew Hunt." Sam told them. "Maggie, do you think we could sit in the porch swing when you finish up the dishes?" He waited to see her nod, "I'll go out with Andie and read her a story while you get done. Come on Andie, you get to choose the one you want me to read!"

"Yippee, Uncle Sam. I know exactly which one I want!" Andie jumped up from the table and raced to get the book of her choice.

"Tessa...would you like...to take a walk with me when you're finished helping Maggie with the dishes?" Reece asked with his heart pounding away.

"I would love to, Reece. It shouldn't be too long. Do you want to wait on the front porch and listen to the story Sam will be reading to Andie? That way I'll know where to find you when I'm done here." Tessa told him with a warm smile.

Silas just sat back in his chair in a very satisfied mood. Maggie was getting her barn rebuilt, and there was romance in the air. Miz Maggie deserved as much happiness as she could get. Yes, Siree, it was all working out just fine!

145

CHAPTER 21

Sam read the story to Andie and sent her up to change into her nightgown. He went up in a few minutes to tuck her into bed for the night. He leaned down and kissed her on her forehead. Small arms circled his neck and she gave him a kiss on the cheek.

"Uncle Sam..." Andie began, "Are you going to marry Maggie?"

"I hope so, Andie. But I haven't asked her yet, she might turn me down. Would you like for us to marry Maggie and stay with her forever?" Sam asked her.

"I love Maggie, Uncle Sam, almost as much as I love you! I'd rather have Maggie as my Ma than anyone in the whole world. I love living here in her house, it feels like I'm living in my own house instead of somebody else's. Do you want me to go with you to ask her?" Andie volunteered eagerly.

"No, short stuff, I think this is something that I have to do on my own. But I do appreciate the help if I need it! Now you settle down and go to sleep, it looks like it's going to be a very busy week with building the barn and canning all those vegetables in the garden." Sam tucked the covers up around her shoulders and winked at her. "I hope to have some real good news when you come down to breakfast tomorrow morning!" They both laughed, and then Sam added, "I love you a lot, Andie. I want you to be as happy as I will be if Maggie says yes to my proposal." He left carrying the lamp with him. Maggie was waiting for him on the front porch in the swing. He could see Tessa and Reece disappearing around the corner of the fence.

146

"Sam, you look so tired. Would you prefer to wait to have our talk after you get some much-needed sleep?" Maggie reached up and pushed Sam's hair out of his eyes. The look she gave Sam was so full of love that Sam had to physically touch her, he wanted her so badly.

Maggie met him with welcome arms and for the first time today, he relaxed in her arms. She met him kiss for kiss and it didn't take long for the touches to start getting out of hand. "Maggie, I love you so much and want to do more than kiss you...We've got to stop while I still can. I won't have your name bandied about that I slept in your bed before we were married." Sam told her as he kissed her once again.

"Sam...I'm not an untried virgin. I've been married before, I know what to expect...I want you as much as you want me. Would it be so wrong if we shared a night of passion because of our love?" Maggie asked him. She didn't want him to think her forward, but she wanted a night of passion with Sam. It all felt like it was too good to be true and that at any moment something was going to happen and spoil it.

"No, Maggie, it wouldn't be wrong at all. I'm so glad that you want me as much as I want you. But before we go anywhere, there's something I want to ask you..." Sam paused. He wanted to do this right, for Maggie's sake. "Maggie McDonald, would you do me the very great honor of becoming my wife? Would you stand beside me in thick and thin, in good times and bad? Would you help me raise Andie and any other children we might have some day?" He looked up to see Maggie silently crying and tears running down her face. When she opened up her eyes, they were filled with stars.

"Oh, Sam, nothing would make me happier than to become your wife and Andie's mother! I was afraid that you might not ask me or that you might have changed your mind!" Maggie kissed him eagerly, "I love you so much!"

"Oh, Maggie, you've just made me one very happy man! When? I'm not letting you off the hook! Let's set a date right now, right here!"

"Well, I would like to make a new dress for the occasion and one for Andie, too! Would it be asking too much to say how about in two weeks?" Maggie asked him laughing. She was so happy she couldn't stop crying.

"Two weeks it will be! That will give us time to spread the word to the whole town. We'll have to make arrangements for food and cake. Is there anything else I need to do?" Sam couldn't quit smiling and kissing Maggie.

"I'll pick flowers from my garden. Do you think that the barn will be done by that time? We could have the wedding right here; that way Tessa and I can cook up a feast for everyone we invite. What do you say?"

"It's agreed two weeks from today, we're getting hitched. Between now and then, I plan on kissing you a whole lot! I'll look into getting the minister here for the occasion and getting us some rings. I want every man in this town to know that you're MY woman and that you're taken!" Sam teased.

Meanwhile, Tessa and Reece were having a very nice stroll down the main street of town. Tessa's hand was clasped securely in the arm of Reece and he wasn't letting her go any time soon. Reece finally said more than one-word answers to her. He told her about becoming a U.S. Marshall and growing up in an orphanage. He told her he always wanted to belong to a family, living at Maggie's and having all of them as his friends, was almost like being a family.

Tess listened and heard the lonely little boy as he talked. She told him about growing up the oldest girl in a household of five daughters. She remembered learning to help with the chores because there were no brothers to do the job. She helped her Ma so much that she stayed behind to help her when she got sick. Her sisters got married and moved away. First her mother died and then her father. But before her father died, she got her teacher's certificate. She started teaching as soon as he was gone. She had a few boyfriends, but nothing serious.

"Tess...how do you feel about me?" Reece asked her. "I've never felt about anyone like I feel about you! I've never been in love, I don't rightly know what love is...I do know that I think about you all the time...I dream about you when I'm sleeping. You make me feel good just being around you. I...want to spend the rest of my life with you by my side." Reece hesitated and stopped right in front of the General Store windows. "Tess, would you marry me and spend the rest of our lives together? If you want to teach, you can teach. If you want me to find another line of work, I'll do it. Could you see yourself being married to me?"

Tess didn't hesitate. She threw her arms around Reece and kissed him full on the mouth! "Oh, Reece, I would love to spend the rest of my life with you! I will marry you and make you a home like you've always wanted! Nothing would make me happier than to be able to wake up to your face every morning for the rest of my life!

Reece grabbed her and swung her around and around and then he kissed her over and over again. He was content for the first time in his life. Together they started to plan. Tess couldn't wait to get back and tell Maggie they were getting married!

It was wonderful to see the happiness in Reece and Tessa's faces as they came back from their walk. They couldn't believe the looks they saw on Sam and Maggie's faces. Something good was going on and they all wanted to share their news. At the same time, Maggie and Tess told each other, "We're getting married!"

Reece and Sam were two very happy men. The two couples started to plan. They decided that it would be a double wedding in two weeks. Maggie would make her and Tessa's dresses and Andie's too. They would have ham and turkey and sweet potatoes, corn and green beans. They would work together on making several cakes, biscuits, rolls, and fresh bread for all their guests to consume. They would decorate with flowers from all around Maggie's yard. The men were responsible for talking to the minister and getting the rings. It was going to be a very busy two weeks!

CHAPTER 22

They were indeed very busy in the next few weeks! Andie was thrilled that Maggie was going to become her new mother. She couldn't keep the smile off her face. She was actually going to belong to a family! Silas was happy as well, Sam and Reece assured him that they wanted him to stay on and continue helping the girls out and keeping an eye on the homeplace while they were gone.

Maggie also started cleaning for the good doctor. She made him a large pot of beef stew with the supplies he had bought and even brought him over a couple of pieces of pie that she had left over from the night before. She scrubbed down the entire two rooms he occupied and then tackled the office and surgery. It was filthy. Maggie not only used lye soap, she used plenty of bleach as well. She took all his dirty clothes and linens back to her house to wash them and hang them out on the lines to dry. She would return them when they were dry this afternoon. Andie helped her by filling the wood bins, drying dishes, and collecting some wild flowers to put on his kitchen table.

Then the ladies worked on finishing up on the garden, while the crew of men were building the barn in record time. Silas and Sam had drawn up some plans that would make it large enough for the chickens, buggy, cow, all the horses, and still leave room for a small workroom for Silas. With ten men working, they had the frame up in two days. Then they divided into two teams. One team worked on putting up the walls, and the other worked on putting on a roof. Then they would put in the loft, stalls, and chicken coup. Silas helped supervising the work. He was a knowledgeable little man.

He made sure that the work was done right, and to his surprise, the men actually listened to him.

Maggie wished there were more than twenty-four hours in a day! She still washed and cooked and cleaned, that was along with cleaning out the garden and canning everything she could get her hands on! In the afternoon while she sealed all the cans of vegetables, her sewing machine was going all the time. She was still making the dresses for the General Store in addition to the wedding dresses she was making.

Reece and Tessa were looking at every empty house in Pine City. They wanted a home of their own. They were very content to stay with Maggie and Sam, but they wanted some privacy too! It was at the end of the first week that they found what they were looking for. A couple houses down from Maggie and a street over from the school, a house was put up for sale. The little old lady that lived in the house was going to live with her daughter in Cheyenne. She wanted the house sold so she could be on her way. It was small, but exactly what they wanted and needed. They bought it immediately and most of the furniture that was already in the house came with the sale. Tessa couldn't believe that after all these years, she would be a wife and living in her own home. Reece couldn't believe that after forty-two years, he had found someone to love him and help give him the home he had desperately wanted all his life.

In Tessa and Reece's spare time, they were cleaning the little house and making it their own. Maggie made her take some of the canned vegetables in her cellar and bags of potatoes, sweet potatoes, carrots, and onions. She was also helping her make the curtains for her new house. They both wanted everything to be ready on their wedding day.

Sam and Reece had gone to the Presbyterian minister to see if he would come for the wedding. He agreed. The next order of business were the rings. Jonah Clark had just what they wanted and in the right sizes. Word was spread to the entire town and Sam rode out to let the Murphy's, Graham's and Drew's know about the date. They wanted all their friends to know about their happiness. Jonah and Olivia wanted to give something to the happy couples that were their friends and customers. They arranged for the same men who played their fiddles at the Fourth of July festival to play for their weddings. Sam and Reece couldn't believe that things kept getting better and better!

Judge Sanders came and tried both Matthew Hunt and Jackson Slaughter. Matthew would only get ten years in the Territorial Prison. The judge went lighter on him after learning that he was instrumental in capturing the other robber and most of the money. Hunt had managed to spend almost five hundred dollars living the high life until he was captured. Slaughter got twenty-five years in the Territorial Prison. Even with one leg, he was vowing to get even with all of them, especially Hunt for being the reason he only had one leg. He didn't accept any of the blame for the loss of the leg, or of getting Scott Lane killed, or of robbing the banks. He was living only for revenge. U.S. Marshalls came and drove them away amid much crying from Marissa Hunt for taking her baby so far away from her. Reece and Sam were glad to see justice being done. They also went out of their way to thank Michael Hunt for making restitution for Maggie's barn and possessions.

"I couldn't live in this town and look my customers in the eye if I hadn't seen the wrong done by my son put right. I'm sorry for all the trouble he caused and the damage. I'm hoping that now that it's all over, the town, and our family will be go back to being somewhat normal again. I thank you for putting in a good word for Matthew with the judge. Ten years is a long time, but not near as long as twenty-five years or the rest of his life. Maybe he'll come out a changed man and be able to start all over again. At least, that's my wish. Good luck on your upcoming weddings. Maggie is a wonderful woman, Sam. She deserves to get a good man after the hell her first husband put her through. I don't know the new teacher, but I think she's getting a fine man in you Reece. Pine City is lucky to have both of you for our law enforcers." Michael Hunt shook both their hands and took his sobbing wife home.

Reece and Sam went back to maintaining justice and law and order for the town. It was good to empty out the jail cells and get back to normal.

With Reece and Tessa moving out and Sam moving into her room with Maggie, she had several rooms to rent out. Maggie and Sam talked about whether they wanted to leave the rooms empty or fill them with boarders. Sam liked the idea of the house just being a house, their house. Maggie liked that idea, too, but she was also practical. The empty rooms could bring in some extra revenue that they could use. The problem was solved for them.

There was a knock on her front door early the next morning. Maggie answered it. She had no idea of who she was seeing on her front doorstep. It was a 'lady' with two small boys.

"Are you Maggie McDonald?" She waited for Maggie's nod before she continued. "Were you the one...married to...Stephen McDonald that got himself killed in a poker game?" She asked.

"I am, why do you ask? And exactly who are you?" Maggie had a chill go up her spine. It was almost like she had a premonition that this woman was carrying bad news or news of something bad that was going to happen.

"Ma'am. I don't want to be the bearer of more bad news, but were you aware that your man had himself a mistress here in town?"

"I was aware that Stephen had several...women...that he spent time with during our married life. It was no secret to me or to the entire town." Maggie told her with some dignity.

"Well, while he was living with you, he got a couple of the ladies pregnant. He always paid for the care of his little bastards, but with him being dead, there ain't nobody been paying for me to take care of them for several months now, almost a year. I'm not in any shape to continue taking care of them. This here little one is three years old. Stephen called him Josh. He thought it funny that he had the children you always wanted and didn't know it. This here baby is six months old. My friend...didn't know she was pregnant with 'ole Stephen's bastard when he died. She died having the whelp. I tried to keep good care of them as long as I could, but I can't no more. Mr. McDonald always said that if something happened to him to take his young'uns to his wife Maggie McDonald. He told us you were a good woman who would see to their upbringing. He...told us he didn't treat you very well, but despite all that you were a real lady who did what was right not what was easy. Will you take the boys, ma'am?" She asked Maggie.

Maggie was overwhelmed by the information that the young woman was telling her. "Won't you come in, Miss...? We'll get to the bottom of this. Andie!" Maggie called. When she appeared, "Andie run over to the jail and get your Uncle. Tell him something has come up and I desperately need him right now." Andie didn't like how pale Maggie looked, and she sure didn't know the people standing on her front porch. Something wasn't right, and Maggie needed her help. She ran as fast as her little legs would carry her.

"Uncle Sam come quick! Maggie said to go get you and to come really quick! Some people came to our door and Maggie's not looking too good!" Andie told him as she was gasping for breath.

"Reece stay here with Andie, I'm going to see what's going on. Is Tess at the house or is she at your house or the school?" Sam asked as he walked to the door. He wanted to know who was in the house in case there was danger. He didn't know what Maggie could want him for, but if she did, he'd go to hell and back for his woman.

155

Maggie was sitting in a chair holding a baby when he walked in the door. Andie was right, she looked very pale and close to tears. "Maggie what's up?" Sam asked her and knelt down beside her chair. He cast a wary eye on the 'lady' and little boy sitting very quietly beside her on the couch.

"Sam this is Miss Carrie from the...from one of the...saloons in the town. She claims that these are Stephen's children." Maggie paused letting that sink in. "She's giving them to me because she can no longer take care of them since Stephen is dead and no longer paying her for their keep. The little boy's name is Josh and the baby's name is Robert, but they call him Bobby." She looked up at Sam, "What do we do now?"

"First we check out her story. That should be easy to do, your husband didn't make his actions secret by any means. I'm surprised that you didn't know about the children. How did he manage that...Miss Carrie?" Sam asked her.

"He paid for a little house outside of town for us to live...That was for Elsie...that was her name and me to live. Elsie was Stephen's...girl, I was just the helping hand she needed. We had us a good life...we didn't have to see any other men...just Stephen. He gave us money every week that I guess he won gambling. When...he died...we stayed in the house until Bobby was born and Elsie died. I kept them as long as I could...but we ain't got no money left...I'm going to work in Big Ed's Saloon. I won't be able to keep care of the boys no more. Since they're not mine, but...Elsie's and Stephen's...I guess they're now yours." Carrie finished. This was a lot harder than she thought it would be. She had hoped that she would just drop the children off at the house and be on her merry way. She was attached to the boys, but she had her own life to think about.

Sam whispered into Maggie's ear, "I'm going to check out her story and be back in a few minutes. Why don't you take them back

156

to the kitchen and give them some tea and biscuits or something? I'll try to hurry." He leaned down and kissed her gently on the mouth and squeezed her shoulder and then he took off to get the answers he needed.

"Josh...Carrie, why don't we go back to my kitchen. I was in the process of baking. You can have some tea and milk and some cookies to eat while we wait for Sam to get back to us." Maggie got up still holding the baby in her arms. She hated Stephen all over again for giving the children she wanted to another woman. If everything the woman had told them was true, could she be a good mother to Stephen's children? Or would she transfer her feelings for Stephen onto his children? She looked down at the tiny infant in her arms and at the sad child holding onto Carrie's hand. No, there was no way she could hold these children accountable for Stephen's sins. They were innocent victims and they needed love and a good home to grown up in. Could she and Sam do that?

CHAPTER 23

Sam went directly to the jail to get Reece to help him confirm or deny Miss Carrie's tale. He sent Andie back to stay with Maggie and told her to help her all she could. He even asked her to get Silas and ask him to stay in the kitchen with Maggie and Miss Carrie. He and Reece split up and got busy checking out her story.

Reece talked to Big Ed of Big Ed's Saloon. He was a huge man with red hair and bulging muscles, but with all his bulk he was surprisingly gentle with his 'ladies'. He was also very protective.

"Yeah, I know Carrie and Elsie. I also knew that coot Stephen McDonald. He wasn't welcome in here after he knocked up Elsie and we caught him cheating at one of the poker tables. Next thing I know, Elsie is living in a cabin not far from town and then Carrie leaves to go help out Elsie. That was three four years ago, I guess. I heard by way of the grape vine that Elsie died giving birth to a second baby. Stephen was scum to my way of thinking, but as far as I know he did try to take care of the girls and his children. I never heard of him mistreating them or the children. Whenever I heard from Carrie, he didn't mistreat them but saw to their needs. Does that answer your questions?" Big Ed asked.

"Yes, it does, Ed. Has Miss Carrie told you that she's coming back to work for you?" Reece questioned.

"She did. She asked me if she still had a job. I told her sure, she's a good worker and the men sure like her, but I also told her that I wasn't having any kids hanging around here. A saloon is no place to raise two little babies. She agreed and told me she was going to take them to Stephen's widow. If I was Maggie McDonald and two little kids showed up on my doorstep from my husband's mistress, I sure as hell wouldn't take them in! You tell Miss Maggie from me, that if I can do anything to help you just let me know. She's a good woman and didn't deserve any of the shit her ex-husband put her through." Ed told Reece. The two men shook hands and Reece went to meet Sam.

Sam had gone out to the little cabin that Stephen had rented. It was little more than three rooms. The place was filthy and poorly equipped to raise two children. There were no toys on the floor and certainly no food in the cabin either. Sam found a goat in the backyard, and he assumed that they had been milking the goat to feed the baby. He saw no evidence of a garden, smokehouse, chickens, or any other kind of animal. He looked through each of the rooms and found no clothes or diapers for the children. The babies would certainly be better off living anywhere but here! He went back to find Reece and talk to him about what he found out. But on the way he stopped to talk to the owner of the little cabin. He needed to find out if Stephen had indeed rented out the cabin for the last several years.

A Mr. Ballard owned the cabin. He confirmed the fact that Stephen rented out the cabin and had for the last almost four years. He said that he never stayed long in the cabin, preferring the town life to living in a small cabin outside of town. He said that he always paid up front and often when he had had winning hands paid for the rent ahead of time. He said that he had paid for the cabin for almost a year before he died. He had dropped off meat once in a while after he died to feed the two women he had living there. Sam thanked him and told him about the goat at the cabin, Mr. Ballard promised to go pick it up, then Sam left for the jail to meet Reece.

"Her story checked out, Sam. Big Ed told me about Stephen and Elsie and later about Carrie leaving to help Elsie out. He didn't have a high regard for Stephen McDonald and had barred him from his saloon for cheating at cards. Carrie is coming back to work for him just as soon as she can take the children somewhere they can be taken care of. He said that a saloon is no place to raise children in." Reece told him.

"Well, I found the cabin and the man who rented the cabin to Stephen. The timeline fits with what Miss Carrie told Maggie. The children are Stephen's, but I don't know how Maggie feels about raising Stephen's bastards. I know she hates her dead husband and with good reason. He did everything he could do to embarrass and humiliate her in the entire lifespan of their farce of a marriage. I will give him credit to keeping his children secret. Maggie's always wanted a houseful of children and for him to give his children to another woman, would have been a bitter pill for anyone to swallow, much less Maggie." Sam explained.

"So, what do you do now?"

"Now, I go talk to Maggie and find out what she wants to do about the situation. We might be filling up those bedrooms faster than we planned on!" Sam slapped Reece on the shoulder and headed back to the house and Maggie.

Maggie had given the Miss Carrie and Josh some cookies and milk. She filled the bottle the lady had with milk and fed and diapered the baby too. Andie was very quiet watching the little boy and baby. She didn't understand what was going on, but she knew that Maggie was very quiet and not at all like her usual smiling self. Silas sat in the rocker watching it all. He didn't like anyone upsetting his Miss Maggie. If Sam wanted him to stay there and make sure that she was all right, he'd sit here all day if need be. Maggie had brought him some coffee and cookies as she served everyone else. She was so glad to see Sam ride back home and tie up Beast to the hitching post outside the kitchen window.

"Sorry, it took me so long Maggie, Miss Carrie. Thanks for watching over everything, Silas, I've got it from here." He watched Silas nod and get up and leave the room. "Andie, this is going to concern you too, so I guess you better stay and listen as well." He watched as she smiled at him and nodded. Then he turned to Maggie. "Everything Reece and I found out checks with her story, Maggie. These look to be Stephen's children. How do you fell about that?"

"You know how I feel about Stephen, Sam, but there's no way I can hold these innocent children responsible for their father's sins or hold them responsible for the circumstances of their birth." Maggie began. Sam watched as she gently put the baby on her shoulder to burp and patted his little back. "How do you feel about them?" She asked softly looking into his dark eyes.

"Maggie, you know how I feel about children. I wanted to be able to fill up those bedrooms to make you happy, I see these two as helping us get a head start on our mission." Sam smiled and gently kissed her. "I say they need a home and we can give them a good one. We'll add to the number as the good Lord provides. Andie wanted us to have a baby, this will help with that wish." He turned to Andie, "How do you feel to having two little brothers in addition to getting a new mother?"

"For real, Uncle Sam!?? I'd love to have lots of brothers and sisters like Kit! Yippee!!" Andie told them all with a shout. Then she ran over and hugged Maggie and the baby and Uncle Sam, and so he wouldn't feel left out she hugged Josh, too. Josh wasn't used to people hugging him. He also wasn't used to people giving him milk and cookies in the middle of the morning. His eyes kept getting bigger and bigger. He had no idea his life was about to change for the better.

"Miss Carrie, Maggie and I will take the children and promise to love them and treat them as our own. We thank you for taking such

161

good care of them all these months. We know it hasn't been easy for you. If there's ever anything that we can do for you, just let us know. We are in your debt." Sam stood up and shook Carrie's hand. She couldn't believe that there were such kind people like this in the world. She could sure understand why Stephen told them to take the children to Maggie should anything ever happen to him. She was satisfied that the children would have a much better life with them, than they ever would have had with Elsie and Stephen. She gave Maggie a pillowcase with a few clothes and diapers for the baby, that was the extent of their belongings, and quietly left. She had a new job to get to and to get on with her life.

Maggie looked at the pitiful pile of clothes left and told Sam that she and Andie would need to go shopping for some clothes for the two and diaper material and bottles. Sam told her to go get whatever she needed. He'd stay with the baby and take care of him. Maggie told her they would take Josh, so they could find the right sizes for him. He was barefoot, and they would need to get him shoes along with everything else. Sam reached into his pocket and gave Maggie some five-dollar gold coins. "Go get whatever you need, Maggie. You might stop at the General Store and see if they have a crib for the baby. I'll stop in later and pick it up and pay for it. And Maggie..." Sam smiled, "I love you and I promise to be a good father to ALL our children!" Maggie kissed him and she and Andie each took one of Josh's hands and walked out the door. Sam was a very contented man.

Andie was so excited to be included in helping to take care of her new brothers. She chattered the entire way to the resale store. "Good Morning!" Maggie greeted the lady running the store. "We have need for clothes to fit young Josh, here and some baby clothes for a young baby about six-months old. We'll need shoes, booties, underwear, a nightshirt, socks, used diapers, and definitely some baby blankets, too. Do you think you have all of the items we need?"

"Absolutely! Just follow me, we'll get you taken care of in nothing flat!" Andie and Maggie took Josh and followed the lady to a section of children's clothes.

"Andie pick out three pairs of overalls or pants. Hold them up to see if they fit and are the right length. I'll see if I can find him some shirts and underwear. Josh, do you like this color or this color?" He didn't talk but he would shake his head or nod. His eyes kept getting bigger and bigger at the things they were buying. They then had him try on some shoes. He loved them and didn't want to take them off! Maggie laughed and told him he could wear them out the store, but first they were going to put on some socks, so he wouldn't get blisters wearing them! Andie found a stuffed bear and gave that to him and he hugged it and held onto it while Maggie put on new shoes and socks. He actually smiled when Maggie found some used blocks and a small wagon. They took it up front to buy it too. After paying, Andie carried the package as they headed for the General Store.

Jonah and Olivia couldn't have been more surprised if Maggie had suddenly sprouted two heads! They had no idea that Stephen had two children by a saloon lady! But they quickly got over their surprise and helped Maggie get the diaper material, extra bottles, some rattles, and a crib. Jonah told her to tell Sam not to bother with coming to get it, he was leaving to go out and pick up some things from some of the ranchers and he would drop it off on his way. Maggie paid with the money that Sam had given her and left smiling. She was going to be the proud wife of Sam Kincaid and the mother of three children. She couldn't believe it! All of her dreams were coming true.

Tessa was holding the baby when Maggie and Andie come home. She couldn't believe all that had happened to her friend in the short time she had been gone to her new home. She told Maggie that Reece was going to start sleeping in the new house starting tonight so they would have a room for the two babies. Maggie hugged her and then she and Andie got busy getting Reece's room ready for the two little boys. Josh kept Maggie in his sight at all times. She was this wonderful lady who had bought him shoes and gave him a stuffed bear and cookies. Life just couldn't get any better than that!

Jonah arrived with the crib and he and Silas carried it up and put it in Reece's room. Maggie and Andie lost no time in making the crib up and ready for the baby. They put him down for a nap after they changed his diaper and put him in clean clothes and booties they had just bought for him. Maggie filled the tub and gave Josh a bath, washing his hair with lye soap to kill any lice he might have. Josh loved splashing in the warm water. He also loved getting dressed in his new clothes. Then he and Andie sat on the floor and played with his new blocks. It was the kind of scene that Maggie always imagined would be going on in her home. Tears came to her eyes as she started filling up bottles and cutting out diapers from the diaper material she just bought. There was too much to get done to stand around getting all sentimental over seeing children playing on her kitchen floor.

CHAPTER 24

It was the first week of August, some of the ranchers and farmers were threshing their wheat fields. Maggie and Sam, and Tessa and Reece had one week before the wedding and too much to get ready! Maggie was still canning from the garden. Tomatoes and beets were ready and coming in great abundance. Maggie had more reason now than ever to fill up her cellar with having three children to feed through the winter. Silas made a small pen in the yard for Josh to play while Andie, Maggie, and Tessa worked in the yard and the garden. Maggie usually put the baby on a blanket beside the play pen to keep him out of trouble as well. Silas was busy with the finishing touches on the barn. They had the walls up, the roof on, the chicken coup built, as well as a new pig pen. Some of the animals were back from the livery, they were still working on the loft and the stalls. Silas was working on his workbench and hanging up all his new tools. He kept a close eye on the work being done to make sure that it was done right. Even Michael Hunt had come by to make sure that everything was being done that he had promised.

The livery man promised to bring back the cows and the horses as soon as the stalls were done. He also told Silas to tell Hunt that several loads of straw and hay would be delivered by the end of the week. He would also bring a new buggy for the replacement of the other one.

Tessa told Maggie that her new house was looking great and loved the new curtains that Maggie had made for them. She and Reece had cleaned it from top to bottom and had even bought a few quilts to make it seem homier. Tessa was looking forward to living in her own home with Reece. She had never been happier. She was also looking forward to teaching in the school this year. Jonah Clark at the General Store and mayor of Pine City told her that her being married didn't change the fact that she could teach, at least until they started on the family they both wanted. So, in addition to helping Maggie with the vegetables in the garden, buying what she needed to finish furnishing her home, and getting her classroom ready for the school year, Tessa didn't have a moment to spare and she wouldn't have it any other way!

Maggie couldn't believe how quickly she fell in love with Josh and Bobby. They seemed to blossom in her tender loving care. The baby was all smiles and giggles when she blew bubbles on his fat little tummy as she gave him baths every morning. Josh had actually started talking a little when he realized that these people weren't going to yell at him for making noise or take any of his new-found treasures away from him. He loved having Andie play with him every day and how gentle she would swing him in the yard. He even liked being held by Sam and rocked to sleep in the evenings. Silas found him a little hammer and he helped Silas and Andie make troughs for the pigs and chickens. He loved the thought that he was helping.

Maggie wished that there were more hours in the day! She was canning enough for their household and the McBride's. After all the help Tessa was giving to Maggie, there was no way that she was going to go away empty handed. Maggie asked Reece to buy some pint and quart jars to fill from her garden and he laughed and got them the same afternoon. Sam and Reece kept bringing back game to put in the smoke house and they agreed that since they were both putting meat in the smoke house, they would both keep taking meat out of it. It was more than big enough for two families. He was also going to keep his horse in their barn. It was cheaper than the livery and closer, too. He had even gotten around to naming his horse. After much consideration, he decided that Pablo was the perfect name for him. Andie agreed.

Maggie was finding it very difficult to sew for the General Store, make up all the diapers she needed for Bobby, finish the wedding dresses and still cook, clean, and care for all the children. She would be glad when she was able to pay back Jonah Clark for loaning her the money for the buggy and horse in the first place and to have the wedding over and done with. She was a nervous twit worrying about the wedding night with Sam. Stephen had found her wanting or he wouldn't have gone to other women. She hoped that Sam wouldn't find that to be true as well. She wanted the kind of marriage that her friends Jonah and Olivia had, and that Mary and Cade Murphy had. Maybe she should talk to Sam about her fears?

Sam was finding it harder and harder to keep his hands off of Maggie. He couldn't wait for the week to be ended to make her his wife. He loved watching her with the children. She was such a loving mother and woman, she took his breath away. He also knew that her experience with Stephen had left her a little gun-shy of getting married again and possibly subjecting herself to all that misery again. He had seen the worry in her eyes when she thought no one was looking. He made up his mind to speak to her tonight before they went to bed.

By dinner time, there were over fifty jars of tomatoes, tomato juice, and beets sitting on the porch to take down to her cellar. Tessa had already taken twenty jars home. Dinner was exceptionally good. Reece still ate dinner with them every evening and breakfast every morning. Maggie sent sandwiches for both of the men at lunch with Sam. Tessa and Maggie gave all three children baths tonight and they were all so tired that they almost fell asleep in the bath tub. It was the perfect opening that Maggie and Sam were looking for.

"Maggie let's sit on the swing and talk." Sam began and took her hand and led her to the porch. Reece and Tessa were going for a walk to talk about what else they still needed to be done at their home before they were married.

"Maggie, I know that Stephen was a no-good jerk. I also know that he put you through the mill in your marriage. I don't want you to be worried that this marriage will be the same. I respect my marriage vows and won't make them lightly. I will never dishonor you or sleep with another woman. The fact is, I can't even work up the urge for another woman, you completely fill up my heart with my longing for you. I will love you and respect you for the end of my days. It's going to be all right, love, I promise." Sam told her quietly with her head on his shoulder.

"Sam, I love you so much...I don't want you to be disappointed in me. I know I can cook and clean and sew and even learn how to be a decent mother to our children, but...Stephen said I was a cold woman. I don't want to be cold to you...I would rather die than have you disappointed in our love-making!" Maggie told him in an anguished whisper. "I made the mistake of becoming aggressive with Stephen the first few times we made love...I promise not to disgust you the same way. Just tell me what you want from me, and I'll do it!"

"Maggie, Stephen was a bastard for making you feel bad for wanting him in bed! I want you to want me in bed as much as I want you! We will BOTH be making love to the other person, not just me making love to you. I want your arms around me and I want you smothering me with kisses! I've heard about men who think that women, respectful women, are supposed to just lie there. They're not supposed to like making love with their husbands. I think that's a load of shit! Women have just as much right as their husbands to want to make love and to enjoy it! I'm going to do everything in my power to make you want me, Maggie, and to make it good for you. I want you to like it as much as I will. Do you believe that, Maggie?" Sam told her while he crushed her to him in a hug.

"OH, Sam, I'm so glad you came to Pine City! I didn't think there were men out there like you! I certainly never thought that I would ever be marrying the kind of man I had always wanted. I do want you Sam! I ache for you to lie beside me all night long and love me in all the ways a man loves the woman he makes his wife...I promise to forget everything I learned from Stephen and begin all over with you. I'm glad we talked tonight. I feel so much better about becoming Mrs. Samuel Kincaid." Sam and Maggie spent the next half-hour enjoying learning about each other.

"Maggie, I think we need to see a lawyer about the three children." Sam told her when they came up for air.

"Three?" Maggie was confused.

"I think it's time that Andie became one of our children in name as well as body. Instead of calling me, Uncle Sam, Papa sounds pretty good. Plus, it'll stop any confusion with Josh and Bobby calling us Mama and Papa. I think that Andie needs a mother and a father more than she needs an Uncle and an Aunt. By going through a lawyer, we'll make it so that no one can ever take the children away from us, but we'll do it the legal way. What do you think?" Sam queried.

"I think I'm marrying a very thoughtful man. I would love for all three children to call me Mama and you Papa. Why don't you talk to Ned Whitaker? He's a good lawyer and I've known him for years." Maggie suggested.

"I'll go in the morning. Now I think we better go to bed, I know how much we have to get done in the next few days. I for one can't wait to call you Mrs. Maggie Kincaid! I also can't wait to love you

all night long!" Sam kissed her again and together they walked
into the house.

CHAPTER 25

Two days before the wedding, Maggie finished the last dress for the General Store, the wedding dresses, making a small shirt for Josh to wear to the wedding, and some small sleepers for Bobby. She delivered the dresses to Jonah and took the time to tell he and Olivia thank you for allowing her to make dresses for extra money for some much-needed supplies. She also explained that with three children, she didn't know if she would still have the time to keep making dresses for the General Store. To her relief, they completely understood. Jonah would still come by for the extra butter and eggs that she had, but families came first, and they knew how much her new family meant for Maggie. She had been waiting to have her own family for ten years!

Tessa and Maggie were still canning tomatoes, cucumbers and carrots. Silas told them he would dig up the potatoes, onions and sweet potatoes after the wedding and before school started, so that Tessa could still help and get some much-needed supplies for winter. But they also had to start cooking for the wedding. Chris and Cam rode in with a load of wood and promised to be back with several more. They also told Maggie that the Murphy wedding present to the Kincaid's and McBride's would be a cooked steer to help feed everybody at the wedding. Maggie was thrilled, now they just had to work on what to serve with the meat. Things had suddenly gotten a whole lot easier. Large pans of scalloped potatoes were cut up and all ready to put into the oven the morning of the wedding. Tessa and Maggie made up large quantities of green beans with bits of bacon and ham. They planned to put out jars of bread and butter pickles, relishes, and lots and lots of slices of bread and butter. Olivia came over and told them she was making the wedding cake and would bring it over on the morning of the wedding. Tessa and Maggie couldn't have been happier. And then the telegram came.

It was from the Territorial Prison in Carson City. Slaughter and Hunt had escaped. Slaughter was a man possessed with revenge, it was all he talked about. The U.S. Marshall's felt that he would be coming back to Pine City to get the vengeance he wanted on the town that took his leg away from him and locked him away for the next twenty-five years. They almost felt that Matthew Hunt was being pressured into helping him. Hunt had been a model prisoner, but he was being terrorized by Slaughter. Slaughter had carved out a peg for his leg and had learned quickly how to walk and almost run with the peg. The first thing he did was track down Hunt in the Prison and beat him to within an inch of his life. Since then, he's done whatever Slaughter told him to do. The Marshalls wanted Pine City and especially Sheriff Kincaid and Deputy McBride to be on the alert for any signs of them. They were armed and dangerous.

Sam and Reece sure didn't want trouble on their wedding day, but they also didn't want to be caught unaware. They posted look-outs at both ends of town and told Michael Hunt that Matthew might be getting in touch with him. He was warned that Matthew was jumping to Slaughter's tune and they would be armed. Michael immediately hired several bodyguards to stand watch over his family and his bank. Slaughter just might try to get back the money he had stolen before.

Silas was put on alert and he was given a rifle and a lot of bullets. He was to watch over Tessa and Maggie and their family. Silas promised that he wouldn't let them down. He'd protect them or die trying! Sam didn't want anyone dying, but he sure didn't want anything to happen to spoil Maggie and Tessa's wedding day. Sam and Reece were constantly checking businesses up and down the streets of Pine City to make sure everyone was safe and hadn't seen the escaped fugitives. Together they rode over the land surrounding Pine City, checking any and all possible hiding places for the two men. They were afraid to sleep, so they took turns staying awake and walking the streets. They were determined that they would surprise the two men rather than being surprised themselves.

Jackson Slaughter and Matthew Hunt were on the run. They had stolen whatever they needed as they ran and hid. Slaughter told Hunt that he would die before going back to prison, and if Hunt messed up, he would take him with him to hell. Hunt was scared. He was afraid of Slaughter and he was afraid of the U.S. Marshalls that he knew were on their trail. He worried they would shoot first and ask questions later. He feared that he would end up dead either way. He didn't like being in prison, but it was better than being dead!

They arrived on the outskirts of Pine City at midnight, the morning of the wedding. They were able to find a place to lie low until dawn. Slaughter's plan was to ride down the main drag of town shooting at anyone who looked sideways at them. He was sure that the Sheriff and the Deputy would hear the shooting and come to investigate, and they would be able to shoot them before they became aware of who was doing the shooting. Hunt thought it a foolhardy plan but was too frightened to speak against Slaughter. He didn't want to shoot anyone!

The town seemed to be busy more so than usual. Something big was going on, but they didn't know what. And then Slaughter heard two men talking about the wedding taking place today between the Sheriff and Maggie McDonald and Tessa Lincoln and the Deputy. In a heartbeat, Slaughter changed their plans. They were going to interrupt the wedding and shoot the unsuspecting bridegrooms before they could enjoy their wedding nights with their new wives! And if they shot a few more people in the crowd, so be it! He laughed just thinking how surprised they would be! He would have the last laugh after all.

The Murphy's arrived early to set up the cooked steer and start slicing the meat, platter after platter were filled and taken to the already heavily laden tables to feed the entire town. Mary, Kit, and Andie strung streamers and flowers all over the backyard. Babies played on blankets and toddlers were confined in the playpen that Silas had made for Josh. Chairs were brought in by the wagon load from the churches all over town. Everybody loved Maggie McDonald and wanted to see her happy.

Maggie's fears seemed to have left her. She wanted to be Sam's wife more than anything else in the world. She also wanted to see him safe. She dressed carefully in her wedding dress, but also slipped her derringer into her pocket. She hated the thought of bringing a gun to her own wedding, but if Slaughter or Hunt showed up and tried to hurt Sam or anyone else, they would get more than they bargained for with the derringer.

Everyone arrived and took a chair while they waited for the wedding to commence. It was warm, but then Wyoming is always warm in August. There were some dark clouds off to the west of town, but it would be some time before they even came close to Pine City. Reece and Sam were standing up on the back porch with the preacher. They were waiting for Tessa and Maggie to join them. The Murphy's were sitting in the front row. Cade held Bobby, Mary held Charlie, and Josh was sitting between Cooper and Cody. Kit was watching all three little boys. Chris and Cam were sitting behind their parents. They sure hoped that the wedding didn't take long, the food smelled and looked delicious and they were starving!

174

But then they were always hungry. They were after all growing boys as their Ma told them and trying to fill them up was a never-ending job.

Sam's first glimpse of Maggie took his breath away. She was beautiful in her ivory dress with puffed sleeves and a satin sash around her slender waist. Little Andie's dress was just like Maggie's and she carried flower petals that she dropped in front of Maggie and Sam and Tessa and Reece. Tessa was dressed in a white eyelet dress similar to Maggie's and Andie's. Reece thought she was the most beautiful bride he had ever seen. He was having a hard time swallowing just looking at her. That beautiful creature was going to be his wife!

They were half-way to the preacher when the shooting started. The men were alarmed, they didn't wear their guns to the wedding, and they wanted to guard their families. Silas was still sitting in the loft looking out on the wedding. He wanted to see the two girls get married, but he also didn't want to relax his vigilance against the two sidewinders coming for vengeance against Maggie's family. He took careful aim...when Slaughter raised his arm to shoot Sam, he pulled the trigger before Slaughter could even blink. Slaughter fell from his horse. Hunt had his gun raised as well, but this time Maggie stepped in front of Sam to guard him and raised her derringer at the same time. She fired and hit Hunt in the arm. He dropped his gun. Malachi Graham and Mitch Drew picked up the two guns and covered the two fugitives until Sam and Reece got to them. You could hear Marissa Hunt crying from the back of the crowd about her baby being shot.

Doctor Mitcham hurried forward to check out Slaughter and Hunt. He pronounced Jackson Slaughter dead and that Matthew Hunt was only hit with a minor flesh wound. They carted the dead body away and took Hunt off to be locked up in the jail. Their

175

horses were given to the livery owner and everyone else settled down for the wedding to continue.

Sam's hands couldn't stop shaking. Maggie had jumped in front of him to protect him from being shot. She could have been killed! He never wanted to be that scared again in his entire life! He had looked down the bore of a gun many times in his lifetime, but he was never so scared when he thought Maggie could be shot and killed. He was going to marry the woman and then strangle her for taking such a stupid chance with her life!

Sam and Reece came back to the back yard after locking up Matthew Hunt. Sam kissed Maggie before they said their vows and told her, "Don't you ever take a chance on your life again or I will throttle you!"

Maggie kissed Sam back and told him, "I would do it all over again if it meant that you were safe!" They were married minutes later amid a lot of cheering and clapping. Both Sam and Reece kissed their wives over and over again. It had been a wedding that no one would ever forget!

Chris and Cam got to eat until they were stuffed. There was food enough for everyone and then the music started. Sam took Maggie and Reece took Tessa out to the middle of the circle and started to dance. It wasn't long before everyone joined in. Silas was slapped on the back and had his hand shook by nearly everyone there. It didn't matter that he was black, he had saved the day for all of them. It was truly a day that everyone wouldn't forget any time soon!!

Maggie kissed Silas on the cheek and then hugged him in front of everyone. Sam and Reece shook his hand and clapped him on the back and called him a hero for saving their wedding from certain disaster! Silas was grinning from ear to ear. Andie brought him a huge plate of food to eat and join the party. Silas sat on the porch and ate his feast. He felt good about helping to give Maggie a wedding she would never forget, but then, neither would the rest of the town!

Thunder sounded in the distance, and many of the families that lived a fair distance from town loaded up and headed for home. The Murphy's, Graham's and Drew's were some of the ones that left. Maggie and Sam made sure that everyone was thanked for attending and gave special thanks to the Murphy's for all the meat they provided. "Sam, put the left-over meat in the smoke house. It should last for several weeks until you can use it up. Congratulations on the wedding and we hope you can be as happy as Mary and I are!" Bobby was put into Maggie's waiting arms and Josh found himself being held in the strong arms of Sam.

The rest of the ladies of the town helped carry all the food into Maggie's kitchen. The men loaded up the tables and chairs and brought them back to the churches they had borrowed them from. Kit and Josie took down all the streamers and ribbons and collected the flowers. Silas helped them put them all in the burn-barrel. He would see to them tomorrow morning. It seemed like in minutes the back yard was back to looking normal again and that's when the rest of the town left to get home before it started to rain.

Reece and Sam took over a plate of food for their prisoner and made sure that he was locked up and everything in town looked good. They didn't want anything to interrupt their wedding nights with their brides.

Maggie put Bobby down for the night after feeding him his last bottle. She helped Josh change into his nightshirt and tucked him in as well. They were both asleep before she turned down the lantern. Then she went to Andie's bedroom. She was already in bed. Maggie kissed her and thanked her for helping to make it such a wonderful wedding.

"Andie, I am so thankful that I will never lose you. I have loved having you become a part of my life. I've already felt that you were like a daughter to me, and now you really are a daughter to me! I will promise to be the best mother I can be to you, Josh, and Bobby! I love you so much! You are the perfect daughter I always wanted!" Maggie was crying by the time she was finished, and Andie threw herself into Maggie's arms.

"If I could choose anyone to be my ma, it would be you, Maggie! I have loved you from almost the first minute we moved in here. I am so glad that my Uncle...my new pa married you. I will love being a part of a real family, even to having pesty brothers! I am so glad that we get to stay here with you forever and ever and I'll never have to be afraid of being left alone again! I love you...Ma!" Andie told her and then kissed her on the cheek. Maggie tucked her in, it was to be the first of many times. Then Maggie went down the stairs to get ready to meet her new husband.

She had made a special nightgown for the occasion. It was made of ivory linen with tiny flowers embroidered along the collar and at the ends of the sleeves. It was simple with its softly flowing fullness and helped make Maggie feel beautiful for her bridegroom. She sat down to brush out her hair. Tonight, she wouldn't put it into a braid, she would leave it down and hoped that Sam would like it that way. Maggie didn't have to wait long before Sam came into the house. He made sure the front and back door were locked and latched. He checked the fire in the fireplace and the cook stove. When he couldn't find anything else that needed his attention, he walked slowly to Maggie's room. His hands shook as he tried the doorknob. Maggie was sitting on the bed waiting for him. His breath caught in his chest, he couldn't get a large breath. Never had he seen anything so beautiful in his lifetime.

Sam walked over to Maggie and pulled her into his arms for a much-needed hug. He held her against him while his heart thundered, and he could feel his blood pumping through his body.

He was already getting hard holding her, how was he ever going to be able to go slow enough to make it good for his new wife?

Maggie started unbuttoning his shirt and untied his string tie. Both dropped to the floor. She ran her hands over his chest and kissed him over and over again. Sam undid his own trousers and dropped them and kicked off his boots. He untied Maggie's nightgown and let it drop to her feet. He bent to remove his short johns, and as he stood back up he picked up Maggie as if she weighed no more than a feather. He laid her down on the bed and his hands traveled over the entire length of her. Never had anything felt so good to him in his entire life. It was like touching satin. Her skin was incredibly soft, her breasts were full and completely filled his hands to overflowing, her waist was tiny, and her hips...were perfect. She had the most incredible long legs. He couldn't stop touching her and kissing her. When he put one of her breasts in his mouth, Maggie thought she had died and gone to heaven. It felt so good to have him touch her as if he had all the time in the world. Maggie's hands began to move over Sam's body. She loved the feel of his chest against her breasts. Her hand moved lower until she touched him. It seemed huge and yet he trembled when she tenderly moved her hand up and down, so big and yet so tender.

Sam didn't know how much longer he could hold himself back. With Maggie's urging, he lowered himself over her and place his penis at the opening of her womanhood. "Maggie, I love you today, tomorrow, and forever from this day on, we are one." Sam whispered as he slowly entered Maggie. Tears rolled down Maggie's cheeks at how good she felt and how wonderful it was making love with Sam.

"Sam, I love you today...tomorrow...and forever from this day on...we are truly one." Maggie answered his whisper with one of her own. Then the age-old ritual took over, Maggie met each of

Sam's thrusts with her own and soon they were both spiraling out of control. Maggie cried out Sam's name when she reached her first-ever climax, and Sam cried out her name as his body convulsed over the women he loved. Sweat covered both of their bodies and they were both breathing heavily.

It didn't matter that a storm came with driving rain and a harsh wind. Throughout the night, Sam and Maggie loved each other and truly became man and wife. They didn't hear the branches that broke loose from the wind or the thundering pitter patter on the roof. They were oblivious as they lay in each other's arms. Sleep finally came to them in the early hours of the morning. It had been a perfect wedding night for both of them.

Morning found them kissing each other as they hurried to dress and be about their early chores. Maggie blushed as she remembered how wonderful Sam had been last night. She made the bed and sighed over the beautiful memory they had made. Then she went into the kitchen to start making breakfast for her hungry family.

Silas and Sam surveyed their property and decided that they survived the storm pretty well. Only a few branches were down, no damage had been done to the house or the barn. Even the smokehouse came out without any problems. Sam started cutting up the branches that had fallen while Silas went in to gather up the eggs, milk the cow and let the animals out for the day.

Others in town weren't so lucky about the storm. Some of the people had damage to their roofs. There were several branches all over the thoroughfare of the town and would have to be cleaned up. But it didn't look like they had any loss of people. Everything else could be fixed or repaired.

Tessa came over after she had seen Reece off to work. She was beaming, so Maggie knew that she had a wonderful wedding night as well. As soon as Maggie could get Josh and Bobby settled, Silas started digging up the onions, potatoes, and sweet potatoes. Andie, Tessa, and Maggie gathered them up and washed them off and put them on the porch and on the tarp that Silas had laid down to dry. It took them most of the day. They only stopped to eat a quick lunch of left-overs and went back to work. Maggie suggested that Tessa and Reece eat dinner with them to help them get rid of all the leftovers they still had in the kitchen. Neither of them wanted the food to go to waste, so she agreed.

By dinner time, Maggie was tired and sore from lifting all the sacks onto the porch. The onions filled almost three sacks, the potatoes filled over five, and the sweet potatoes filled another three. They would leave carrying them down to the cellars to their husbands. Maggie suggested that they use her buggy to carry all the bags to Tessa and Reece's new home, and Tessa jumped at the offer. She also thanked Maggie and Silas for all the vegetables that she now had to help them get through the winter.

Together they went in to feed Bobby and to get their dinner ready for the men to come home. Silas went to feed and water the animals and to bed them down for the night. He would also milk the cow. It was a very mellow time in the Kincaid household.

Reece and Sam came in together and they were as tired as the two women were. They had spent all day helping to patch up the roofs of those that needed it and to remove all the branches that seemed to clog up the streets. They had used the chopped-up wood to lay against the jail house wall, it would help keep it warm through the winter months. They had telegraphed the U.S. Marshalls office with news of Slaughter's death and Hunt's capture. They would be coming in the next day or so to take him back to prison. They also had ridden out to make sure that their friends had made it back to their ranches before the heavy rains had fallen. They wanted to double-check and make sure that they survived the storm with relatively few problems.

They had found Chris and Cam chopping wood from the branches that had fallen. Kit, Cooper, and Cody were dragging every branch and stick that they could find to help clear the yard. It had been too wet for them to thresh the wheat, so Cade found himself helping Mary dig up the potatoes, onions, and sweet potatoes from their garden as well. When the children finished clearing the yard, they would help wash and put the vegetables into burlap sacks to carry to the cellar. Charlie was happily laying on a blanket shaking a rattle. It was a good peaceful scene. Reece and Sam didn't stay long, they had others to check up on and they were in a hurry to get back to town and to their new wives.

Even with the rain, it was very warm and very dry. The rain had soaked into the ground and helped give the brown grasslands new life. You could see green again even from the short time it had fallen. "Reece the rain looks like it helped the dryness, but I still worry about a wildfire. I want every rancher and farmer in the area to make a dirt break around their buildings. It's the only thing that will help them survive if a fire starts. We'll tell them to make it about twenty feet wide, so the fire can't jump over it. It shouldn't take them too long to do it and it won't make any difference if we don't need it, but it could mean the difference between life or death if we get a fire. Let's split up and we'll be able to spread the word a lot easier. Then we have to have the town do the same thing. We need a cushion if there is a fire so that we can stop the fire before it destroys the entire town. It looks like we'll be busy for the nest few days." Reece agreed, and they split up and set out.

Everyone agreed with Sam. They would rather be safe than sorry. It took them several days to get the trench dug around the entire town. Most of the ranchers and farmers made the trench before they went out to finish thrashing and cutting their crops. Several times they saw storm clouds off in the distance, but none of the rain made it to Pine City. Most of the fields had been cleared, cut, thrashed, and stored when they encountered another storm. This one had a lot of lightening. They feared that it would only take one spark to set things off. They were right!

CHAPTER 26

The lightning split a huge oak and sent sparks in every direction at once. Even with the rain falling, a blaze erupted. The ground was so dry it started eating up trees throughout the woods. The woods bordered the ranches of the Murphy's, Graham's and Drew's. All through the night, the fire spread. The fields had been threshed and cut, but they had left behind the short stubs of the dried shafts of wheat, oats, and corn. All of it helped feed the hungry fire. It didn't take long before the fire started encroaching on the buildings of the ranches.

All three families were huddled in their cellars. Wet cloths were placed over their faces to help keep them from breathing all the smoke. Never had the families been so glad to have taken the time to make the fire break around their entire homestead. They might lose wood from the woods and their land might be scorched, but their crops were gathered and stored, and their families were safe. Cade worried about his herd of cattle. He hoped they had the good sense to cross the creek and get to safe ground. But his family was safe, and that was the most important thing in his mind. He met Mary's eyes across the cellar and even managed a smile. They would survive. But they worried about their neighbors and the town. Would they be as lucky?

Reece saw the smoke even before they knew that there was a fire coming straight to the town. He called the alarm. Men started making an even wider fire break around the town. Others were throwing bucket after bucket of water on the roofs of every building in town. Animals were put safely in barns and women and children went to cellars to wait out the fire. Maggie had Tessa, Silas, and the children with her in the cellar. They had wet cloths over their faces and Maggie kept one over Bobby as he slept through it all. Maggie worried about Sam, Tessa worried about Reece, and they all thought about all their friends and families out in the fire's path. They both prayed for the safety of all of them.

The fire break and the buckets of water saved the town from certain destruction. Black soot covered much of the town's walls and roofs, but the fire had managed to burn around them. It was finally stopped when it came to the river west of town. It took three days, but it eventually burned itself out. The good thing about the fire was that it cleared out a lot of the broken limbs and dead wood in the woods and surrounding areas. By the time spring came to Pine City, you wouldn't even know that a fire had almost burned down the town. Many thanks were given to Reece and Sam for having the foresight to making the firebreaks in the first place. The town wasted little time before they were out washing down the soot off the buildings and getting things back to normal.

School started, and Tessa had her hands full with almost thirty children in her one room schoolhouse. Chris, Cam, and Kit Murphy rode their horses in the morning and home again at night every day. They were joined by the three Graham children, Rose, Dylan and Lily, and also the Drew children, David and Emma. Andie couldn't hardly wait to join all her friends at school. Thanks to Maggie, she knew her alphabet and her numbers. And she could proudly write her name.

Maggie settled down into making Reece's room into a bedroom for Josh and making Tessa's room into a bedroom for Bobby. She had enough furniture for both rooms, but she wanted to make the curtains and bedspreads geared more for children than adults. Every day while the children took their naps, she worked on her sewing machine. It was a labor of love doing for her family and she couldn't have been happier.

Their first snow came at the end of August. It only snowed about a foot, but it made Maggie realize that she needed much heavier coats for Josh and Bobby, and her entire family needed goulashes, gloves, and knit hats for the winter. She went into high gear making warm winter coats and knitting gloves, hats and scarves. She bought leather gloves for Sam and Silas with her butter and egg money. Within two weeks, everyone had warm woolen mittens, gloves, scarves, and thick coats. Josh loved playing out in the snow with Andie. Sam helped him make snowballs and let him throw them at his sister. Andie loved it! She had never had many children to play with before and now she had a little brother that wanted to play with her all the time. She loved going over to Josie's house after school or having Josie come over to her house. It was so much fun to invite her up to her room and they could play with their dolls or cut out paper dolls from the catalogs that Josie's father furnished. Maggie would bring up hot chocolate and give them cookies to eat. It was everything Andie had dreamed about when she wished for a forever house and a real live mother.

Maggie and Sam sat down and planned what they wanted to get the children for Christmas. They included Silas, because he was so good at working with wood. They soon enlisted his aid in making sleds for Andie and Josh, a doll house for Andie, and a rocking horses for Josh and Bobby. Sam found little toy soldiers for Josh, more blocks for Bobby, and a tea set for Andie. He also bought a cameo broach for Maggie. Maggie bought enough material to make several dresses for Andie, shirts for Josh, Silas, and Sam, and even more yarn so she could make a shawl for Mary, Olivia, and Tessa. She found a pocket watch for Sam and a pocket knife for Silas. They couldn't wait for Christmas to get there so they could give all the presents to their friends and children. But before they could get to Christmas, they still had Thanksgiving to get through. Maggie and Sam wanted everyone to come to their house for the feast that she had planned. It would be the first dinner Maggie would be having with her new family and friends. Last year, she spent it with the Murphy's, her sister, and Lily and Wes Peters. She couldn't believe how much things had changed in just a little over a year!

A year ago, she was a recent widow, not knowing what she was going to do to make enough to keep the house and make a decent living for herself. Then the Sheriff and his deputy came with his niece! What a difference they had made in her life! Then they found Silas and he became part of her family. Maggie didn't know what she would do without Silas, and she didn't want to find out. He had been a god-send to her and the Kincaid's. He had been the muscle she needed to get the chickens, pigs, cow, cellar, and smokehouse going. Then came little Josh and baby Bobby, what a difference they made on their lives. Never had Maggie thought that she would be the mother of three wonderful children and married to the most amazing man. She hadn't thought she would ever take the plunge and get married again after the fiasco with Stephen. But Sam was like night and day different than her first husband was. This was how she had envisioned her life to be like as she was growing up. Her dreams had always included her having lots of children and a husband that loved her deeply and that she loved in return. She never thought her dream would come through after the last nine years married to Stephen.

The adoptions for all three children had finally come through. The three children were officially Joshua Reece Kincaid, Robert (Bobby) Silas Kincaid, and Andrea (Andie) Rebecca Kincaid. Josh was a different child from the silent waif that had first come to them. He was a happy, laughing child who loved to play with his older sister when she came home from school each day. He loved to get and give hugs and kisses to all of his family. Bobby was fat and giggled all the time. He was just starting to walk and get into everything! He called Sam and Maggie Ma-Ma and Da-da much to their delight. Andie was in seventh heaven. She was finally apart of the family she always wanted to be with. She loved her new mother and loved calling Sam Papa.

It was truly a new day when Sam arrived in Pine City. It was a new start for both of them and a much better life for their entire family. God had certainly blessed her, he hadn't forgot about her after all.

EPILOGUE

A year has passed since Maggie and Sam married. The town, their family, and their friends have had a very good year. Maggie is awaiting the birth of her baby. Sam can hardly get his work done, he keeps coming home to check up on her. He and Silas are making sure that she doesn't over do it working in the garden and taking care of the other three children. Josh is big enough to help this year picking the ripe vegetables with Andie, and Bobby has grown big enough to be put into the little play pen they had used with Josh. Tessa still helps with the garden and together they split the vegetables with Maggie's family.

They acquired more chickens and a few more pigs to fatten up when the weather gets cold. Beauty had a caramel colored foal at the beginning of the summer and Andie loved taking care of it. She had named her Honey and Sam let her. They both felt that when the foal was big enough, she would be Andie's. Silas had never been happier. For the first time he could remember, he had a home and was a valuable member of the household. He loved Maggie and all the children. Maggie had them calling him Grandpa before he could object, and he loved it. Silas and Sam took care of the animals and the buildings. Sam always talked over with Silas before they made any decisions about the household that would require him doing any more work. He depended on him to look out for his family when he was away at work. They often smoked their pipes on the back porch at night before they went to sleep.

Maggie had helped several women give birth in town, but she had never been pregnant before. She knew what to expect, but she didn't know how she would handle the labor and the pain. She didn't want to make it harder on Sam by watching her be in labor. She almost wished that he would be called away for most of the labor and only get back when it was almost over. She wanted to spare him the worry over her and the baby. They talked about names every night when they went to bed. But they hadn't really decided on which one they were going to use.

Maggie's water broke while she was washing off the potatoes that Silas had dug up. Andie and Josh were carrying them from the garden to the wash stand. Tessa was carrying them to the porch after they were washed. Everyone just stood there for a minute as they watched a puddle form around Maggie's feet. Then Silas and Tessa went into high gear. Silas took over the care of the boys, Andie took off to let her Pa know that Maggie was in labor. Tessa helped Maggie get into the house and change out of her wet clothes into a comfortable nightgown. She also put down the oil cloth and newspapers to help keep the mattress dry. Everything was then covered with clean sheets. Maggie washed in the tub to make sure she was clean, and then and only then, did she let Tessa talk her into lying down.

Sam arrived with Olivia to help her deliver the baby. Sam was a nervous wreck. He didn't know what to do to help. Maggie's labor pains had started, and they were strong and about five minutes apart. That was good, hopefully it meant that Maggie's labor wouldn't be too long. Sam sat beside Maggie and helped her take short breaths during the contractions and longer cleansing breaths between contractions. Tessa and Olivia busied themselves boiling water, getting garments for the baby to wear, heating up bricks for the cradle to keep the baby warm, and making food for the rest of the family to eat.

Sam didn't know how long he had been sitting beside Maggie and holding her hand, when suddenly the contractions got much harder. He couldn't believe how hard Maggie was grabbing hold of his hand. He wondered if he would ever be able to pull the trigger again after the baby was born! Maggie was pushing and bearing down trying to expel the baby from her body. She was covered in sweat, but she didn't utter a sound. Sam was ready to cry, but Maggie was not. She had a job to do and she was going to do it. She was having the baby she always wanted. She couldn't wait to hold the fourth child in their family. She knew that she couldn't love this one any more than the other three that completely captivated her love from the first time that she had seen each and every one of them.

"Maggie! I see the head...just a couple big pushes and you'll be holding the newest member of your family. Sam get behind Maggie and support her as she pushes this child into the world." Olivia was giving orders right and left. She was perfectly calm except for the slight trembling of her hands. She wanted everything to go right with this birth. Maggie was the best friend she had ever had.

"That's it Maggie...one more push. Look at all that dark hair...I've got him! It's a boy! Maggie...Sam...you have a good sized little boy! Let Tessa and I clean up the baby and you Maggie and then you can hold him and count all his fingers and toes! He's just beautiful..." Olivia told her amid the tears that streamed down her face. She was so glad that everything was all right.

Baby Kincaid was crying and wiggling all over as Tessa washed him up and dressed him in a sleeper, diapers, and booties. Olivia cleaned up the afterbirth and dirty papers and washed Maggie's tired limbs. She put her in a clean nightgown and put down clean sheets as Sam lifted up Maggie and held her while she finished up cleaning up the bed.

191

Sam felt like he was holding the entire world in his arms. Maggie was his life. He loved her beyond all reason, he just knew that he didn't know what he would ever do without her. He kept kissing her forehead, her nose, her lips and telling her over and over again how very much he loved her. Maggie was taking a nap. She was so tired, and she felt so euphoric. She had given Sam another son. She opened up her tired eyes and smiled at Sam.

"So...Papa, what are we going to name our newest son?" Maggie whispered to him as Sam laid her back down on the clean bed. "I love you Sam..."

"I love you Maggie Kincaid! How does the name Jonathon Samuel Kincaid sound to you? He's not a junior with the same name as me, but he will carry my name for his second name. My father's name was Jonathon...I'd like to honor him by naming our son after him." Sam told Maggie.

"I think it's perfect...just like his father. Can I hold our son now?" Maggie asked.

Into her waiting arms, Jonathon Kincaid was placed. He was chewing on his fist and Maggie knew that it wouldn't be long before she would need to feed her little son. He was the perfect way to end the day.

The End

Note from the Author

I want to personally thank you for your time and effort in the reading of this book. I love writing, and I owe it to my readers to do the best I can. The best source of input to influence my future efforts is your feedback. Please take just a few minutes to share whatever thoughts you may have on this book by going to https://www.amazon.com/author/m_dipaolo and submit a rating and, if you wish, some comments as well. I would really appreciate it.

ABOUT THE AUTHOR

Marcella (Marky) DiPaolo was raised as a farm girl in Moro, Illinois. She was one of six children, and they all interacted daily with their loving parents and grandparents who served as ideal role models for them as they grew up on the farm. Upon graduating from high school, Marcella started her career in business. She also went to college, initially to become an accountant. It was in the business world that she met the person with whom she wanted to share the rest of her life.

It didn't take long for the young couple to start filling up their home with children. It was in the raising of her own that she realized that working with kids was her passion. She decided that teaching was the direction she wanted to go. During the early years, she was the one that stayed home to watch the kids while her husband worked during the day and went to school at night to complete his education. Once finished, he spent his evenings with the children, so she could go on and complete her BA in Elementary Education and later getting a Masters with a concentration in mathematics.

After more than thirty-five years of teaching, she recently retired but continues to teach from time to time as a substitute at a local parochial school. Over the years, Mrs. D., as she is referred to by her students, was recognized for her teaching accomplishments having received several awards and other forms of recognition. 'Mrs. D' has certainly had a very special effect on a lot of young people, all of whom she still considers members of her 'extended' family.

Marcella has a lot of other interests as well. In addition to a voracious appetite for romantic plots and characters, she is also fond of adventure stories and mysteries. She also loves to watch sports, play golf, eat chocolate, and spend as much time as possible with her family.

Marcella's love of reading began at a very early age. However, she never dreamed she might become a writer until much later in life. Being somewhat addicted to historical romances, both in books and on the screen, she has been exposed to a lot of writing styles. This experience and her time on the farm, raising a family, and all those years in the classroom have provided her with a wealth of ideas to apply to her writing career.

Other Books Written by Marcella DiPaolo

Clear Water Bride Series
   Bargain Bride
   Troubled Bride
   Forgotten Bride
   Reluctant Bride
   Runaway Bride

Morgan Brothers Storm Series
   Above the Storm
   After the Storm
   Beyond the Storm

SERIES OVERVIEW

TAKING A CHANCE

Mary Williams has lost her husband, her young son, and both parents in less than a year. She is constantly haunted by the memories of all that she has lost. She decides she needs to leave St. Louis and start over somewhere new, someplace where she can make a difference.

Cade Murphy lost his wife of twelve years a few months ago. He's left with five children and a ranch to take care of. He can't do it all alone. He sends away for a mail order bride, but not too many women want five children when they tie the knot. If Cade doesn't find a wife pretty soon, he may lose the ranch he and his late wife spent years building. He can't spend all his time planting crops and looking after all his children.

One of Cade's friends in Pine City, Wyoming is Maggie McDonald. Maggie has a sister, Brenda, in St. Louis and she just happens to know Mary Williams and her situation. The two sisters decide to play matchmaker. When Cade finds out about Mary from Maggie, he jumps at the chance that might turn out to be the first good thing to happen to his family in many months.

Mary decides to plunge ahead and help him and his motherless children. They both decide that the marriage will be in name only. They both loved their spouses and don't want a real marriage. Time and circumstances will decide their future happiness. Will they both find a new love to change both their lives and that of his five children forever? It could be Taking a Chance for all of them.

A SECOND CHANCE

Maggie McDonald married what she thought was the man of her dreams ten years ago. They bought a house with lots of rooms that she wanted to fill up with lots of children. By the end of their first year of marriage, Maggie finds out that Stephen, her husband, is not the man she thought he was. He's a gambler, a con man, and a cheat. Maggie throws him out of her bedroom and turns her huge home into a boarding house. Later Stephen gets shot over a poker game.

For various reasons, Maggie loses all her boarders and then gets to start over with new and different boarders. They were different because, unlike the former renters that she barely knew, she became closer and more involved in the lives of her new tenants. For example, the new Sheriff, his niece, and his deputy move into her boarding house. They open up a whole new world for Maggie and the new life she wants to have.

Sam Kincaid has been a U.S. Marshall for over fifteen years, recently his brother died in a fire. His niece was one of the few survivors. He needs a stable home for his niece to grow up in. Mrs. McDonald seems to be just the person for Andie, his niece, to get to know.

Maggie's new boarders feel more like family than strangers, and soon a new relationship grows between Sam and Maggie. A Second Chance brings all sorts of surprises to Maggie's Boarding House, and shows her that she should never give up on her dreams.